Rules for Savannah and Jackson's Courting
(Mama actually wrote this!)

1. Y'all are not to be alone in the house together under any circumstances. This goes for the Channings' house, too.

2. When at either house, the bedroom door is to remain open at all times.

3. The back of the Channing boys' truck is off-limits— period!

4. Y'all are not to be out at the beach after dark.

5. Savannah's curfew is 10 o'clock during the week and 11 o'clock on weekends. *(Like it would even matter whether it's the week or the weekend during summer vacation!)*

6. Savannah may spend time with Jackson only after her chores are done. *(I knew that one was coming.)*

7. Finally, y'all best mind your manners. I've got eyes watching for me just about everywhere. Don't cross me.

OTHER BOOKS YOU MAY ENJOY

Breathing

CHERYL RENÉE HERBSMAN

speak

An Imprint of Penguin Group (USA) Inc.

SPEAK
Published by the Penguin Group
Penguin Group (USA) Inc., 345 Hudson Street, New York, New York 10014, U.S.A.
Penguin Group (Canada), 90 Eglinton Avenue East, Suite 700, Toronto, Ontario, Canada M4P 2Y3
(a division of Pearson Penguin Canada Inc.)
Penguin Books Ltd, 80 Strand, London WC2R 0RL, England
Penguin Ireland, 25 St Stephen's Green, Dublin 2, Ireland (a division of Penguin Books Ltd)
Penguin Group (Australia), 250 Camberwell Road, Camberwell, Victoria 3124, Australia
(a division of Pearson Australia Group Pty Ltd)
Penguin Books India Pvt Ltd, 11 Community Centre, Panchsheel Park, New Delhi - 110 017, India
Penguin Group (NZ), 67 Apollo Drive, Rosedale, North Shore 0632, New Zealand
(a division of Pearson New Zealand Ltd.)
Penguin Books (South Africa) (Pty) Ltd, 24 Sturdee Avenue,
Rosebank, Johannesburg 2196, South Africa

Registered Offices: Penguin Books Ltd, 80 Strand, London WC2R 0RL, England

First published in the United States of America by Viking,
a member of Penguin Group (USA) Inc., 2009
Published by Speak, an imprint of Penguin Group (USA) Inc., 2010

1 3 5 7 9 10 8 6 4 2

THE LIBRARY OF CONGRESS HAS CATALOGED THE VIKING EDITION AS FOLLOWS:
Herbsman, Cheryl.
Breathing / by Cheryl Herbsman.
p. cm.
Summary: With a new boyfriend, asthma attacks that come when least expected, and a pesky younger
brother, fifteen-year-old Savannah's summer vacation takes many unexpected twists and turns.
ISBN: 978-0-670-01123-0 (hc)
[1. Dating (Social customs)—Fiction. 2. Asthma—Fiction. 3. Brothers and sisters—Fiction.
4. Interpersonal relations—Fiction.] I. Title.
PZ7.H4311Br 2009 [Fic]—dc22 2008023262

Speak ISBN 978-0-14-241601-3

Printed in the United States of America

Set in Minion
Book design by Sam Kim

To Oded,
for always holding the dream.

And to Maya and Jonah,
our dreams come true.

1

Strange feelings come over me sometimes, kind of like déjà vu, only before it happens. It's sort of like I know what's heading my way, but not really. I reckon some folks would find that peculiar, but I'm used to it by now. Up out of nowhere came the feeling this very morning that this'll be the summer I remember as the one when everything changed.

But first off, let me loop back around and start at the beginning. Savannah Georgina Brown is the name my mama chose for me, according to her family's tradition. At the moment I came slithering out of her body, she cut on the radio and named me for the first word she heard—as if it was a sign from above. That's how her kin have chosen their babies' names going back for generations. Apparently, when I was born, the newsman was going on about a tornado that was hitting Savannah, Georgia. But Mama thought naming me Savannah Georgia Brown would be tacky. So it's Savannah Georgina Brown. Like that's so much better.

I'm just relieved I didn't come out one second sooner, or my name might have been Tornado Brown. Or what if that durn storm had been headed towards Augusta or worse yet, Macon! Alls I can say is thank the Lord it was a tornado and not a hurricane—'cause them hurricanes always end up with old lady names like Henrietta or Pearl.

My daddy gave me my last name—after himself, of course—Brown. That's about all I got left of him, that and a pair of lungs that quit on me every time the wind blows. The way Mama tells it, my asthma started the very day he left us. Supposedly his name is Booker Bo Brown III, and those who know him call him Trip. Sadly I can't count myself among them, seeing as how he *tripped* right on out of our lives when I was barely out of diapers.

"Savannah!" Mama's hollering at me now.

"Yes'm?"

"Where in the you-know-what is your brother at?"

"How should I know? Am I his keeper?"

"Damn right you are! Now hustle on down to the beach and tell that boy to come do his chores like I asked him. I've got exactly ten minutes to get my butt to work 'fore they fire my ass. I haven't time to be chasing him all over tarnation!"

"Like I do?" I mutter. "Why's it always me has to be on him?"

Mama's been fired from near about every job in town. Aside from being consistently tardy, which she just can't seem to help, she has to miss work a lot. They don't take too kindly to that. It ain't as if it's her fault.

"Did you hear me, girl? Now quit running your mouth and go on after your brother!"

"Yes, ma'am." I guess I'm headed to the beach. Least I can take my bike. By the time they're going into the tenth grade, most girls think riding a bike is dumb or babyish, but not me. I love riding fast and free, wind blowing in my ears. I could ride all day if Mama would let me. It don't take but five minutes to get down to the beach the back way.

Anyhow, like I was saying, my daddy cut out on us when I was three, right after Dog was born. Dog's my little brother. Mama named him Dogwood after the tree that was blooming outside her window when he was born. After my close call with the tornado, and with my daddy on the verge of leaving, that's how scared she was to see what sign the heavens might send. Personally, I think the radio would have been a better bet. I mean, dogwoods are pretty and all with their tender white flowers reminding you that spring is nigh, but nobody calls my brother anything but Dog. Can you imagine? He thinks he's got the coolest name on God's green earth. I tell you what—I feel sorry for him come fall when he hits the seventh grade and comes to find out it's one big joke. What kind of sane person wants to go about with a name like Dog? At least he ain't a girl.

I'm almost down to the beach. We live in an itty bitty town on the Carolina coast. Hardly nobody even knows it's here—unless they need some gas or a bite to eat, and get a little lost. Not like one of them tourist towns where all the beachgoers end up.

Summer is about the only time of life worth discussing around here. The rest of the year is one big blob of boredom getting in the way of summer vacation. Our town is so dead in wintertime you'd have thought the whole lot of us had got up and took off for some revival meeting or something. Dead as a dang doornail.

I get to the beach, and there's Dog wrestling in the wet sand like a young'un half his age—I swear! "Dog! Get on up outta that mud! Mama says you best get on home and do your chores."

"Has she left for work?"

"Yes! Now git!"

"Then how's she gonn' know what time I come in?"

He has a point. "Just see to it them chores get done 'fore she gets home."

He's already back to wrestling with his sidekick, Davis Wilson, AKA Dave. It ain't exactly a fair fight, since Dog is big for his age and thick like a football player, while Dave is more of your basic runt. Dog and Dave have been best friends as long as I can remember. They're like twins, but from different mothers. They were born one day apart and have spent near about every day since then together. Mama and Gina, Dave's mom, have traded off babysitting since the very beginning.

Once we got big enough not to need a grown-up looking after us, it became my job to watch Dog and Dave in the summers. But this year, Mama and Gina are letting them be out on their own, long as they stay out of trouble. I reckon they're hoping the boys will keep each other busy enough that they won't find their way into too much mischief. Some of their friends go to day camps, but others are in the same boat as us—not having enough money for such things. So they've got plenty of kids to hang around with.

I'm fixing to sit down on the dry sand and enjoy the sun on my face when I spy this surfer I've been keeping my eye on the last couple weeks. He's got short-cropped hair and sea-green eyes. He is so cute.

He looks right sad, though, standing by his board near the shoreline, staring off like there's something waiting for him out there in the water. Lord have mercy, he must have sensed me watching him. He's looking right at me, his eyes connected to mine like he knows me, even though we've never spoken a word. I'm getting all flushed, like I'm the one who's been in the sun all afternoon without protection instead of my stupid brother.

Goodness, I'm smiling at him. How can you not when someone looks at you like that, his eyes all shiny like he's glad to see me? Whoa man, I'm getting worked up. My face must be red as a hornet's hairy behind. I've got to turn away. Not that I want to—I don't—but I mean, I have to. John Brown it, where is my bike? Okay, I caught my breath, I'm going to look back at him. Hell in a handbasket, he's gone.

I think I'll head down the beach a ways, see if I can't see where he got off to. "Dog, I'm warning you!" I yell. That ought to suffice. Anyhow, as I was saying, Mama and Gina have been friends ever since they were both working at the Piggly Wiggly. They kept on trading babysitting even after Mama got fired and started working at the Hardee's. That was quite a few jobs back. Now she's at the Family Dollar Store, which is two towns over. They'd have made her a manager by now if she was more dependable. But like I said, it ain't like it's her fault.

I got serious asthma, and sometimes it gets real bad and I need to go to the hospital, which is a ways from home, and when it's real, real bad Mama's got to carry me clear out to Wilmington for the right doctors. She may leave us alone at home near about every day, but she don't never leave me at the hospital by myself. Mama don't trust them folks any further than she can throw them. When we go in, her little notebook comes out, and down go all the doctors' orders and nurses' names, all to make sure nobody gives me the wrong medicines or nothing.

Maybe her bosses would be more understanding if she'd just tell them why she's not coming to work. But she says she don't want nobody pitying me, that she's had enough pity to last her a lifetime and just can't take no more. Course she won't ever explain what pity it is she's speaking of, no matter how many times I ask her.

Since my asthma started the day my daddy left us, Mama always used to say as soon as he'd come back I'd be free of it. She don't say that no more, though. For a long time, I dreamed about trying to find him. What father could refuse a daughter who can't breathe without him? But in time, I came to find out that this here's a mighty big world. And even if I did track him down, he ain't coming back. He don't care nothing about me, and he never will. He's been gone twelve years with nary so much as one single solitary phone call. No matter. I'll find my own cure. I don't need him for nothing.

The swells are mighty high today. My heart's beating real fast 'cause I see my surfer up ahead. He's new around here and seems to be older than me and my friends. He looks real smart, like he's always thinking about something important. I heard some kids at the snack shack say he's kin to the Channings, which explains why he's always hanging around with them. They live over by the old railroad station. There ain't no trains anymore, though. That area has been developed to look real clean and pretty, so the rich folk have taken it over.

Shoot, he's met up with his cousins. They're a couple years ahead of me in school, super snobby, and mean as one-armed paperhangers with the hives. I guess I best get on to work anyways.

My summer job is at the public library. It ain't but fifteen hours a week, and they only pay subminimum wage, seeing as I'm a student and all. But at least I get to choose my own hours. My main task is reshelving books. Plus sometimes I have to read stories to the little kids, but that's only for twenty minutes or so. Then they leave—not like with babysitting, where you've got to entertain them for hours on end. I don't mind story time when the young'uns are real cute and clap their hands like I did an amazing magic trick just by reading to them. But some days those children give me a headache, when they act like they're sitting on ant hills, screaming and jumping about.

It may sound dorky, but I love books—the feel of the paper, the old, musty smell, and especially the way the words roll over you and take you somewhere altogether different. They've been my escape long as I can remember. Whether I need a break from schoolwork or my brother or just life in general, there's always a book that can take me someplace far away.

"Hey, Miss Patsy," I say to the librarian, after locking my bike out back.

"Hello there, Savannah. We've got quite a few carts waiting on you, and story time starts in forty-five minutes." Her poofy gray hair is standing up rather taller than usual today. She heads into the back room, her weight causing her to go slowly, the silver bangles she wears on her wrists jangling.

"Yes, ma'am," I reply. Miss Patsy has been recommending books to me since I first started reading. Sometimes when a new book comes in, she'll set it aside for me to borrow before it even gets shelved.

It's dead quiet in here today, so I get busy putting up the books. After finishing the children's returns, I start shelving in the young adult section. I come across a copy of *Stallion of My Heart* and flip it open to somewhere in the middle. Before long, I'm hunched down in a corner rereading it. I only meant to look at a page or two.

"Savannah Brown," Miss Patsy scolds, "you are not getting paid to read."

I can usually hear her coming from the clanking of her bracelets as she meanders down the rows. Somehow I managed to miss it today.

"Sorry." I blush, hating getting caught at anything.

"The children are waiting. Then you have two more carts to do."

I hadn't even noticed the hustle and bustle of kids and parents coming in for story time. I scoot into the children's area and sit in the chair up front. There are about fifteen preschoolers bouncing off the walls. It seems more like fifty, they're making such a racket. I start reading *The Very Hungry Caterpillar*. Kids usually love that one. Personally, I think they just like to imagine themselves being able to eat all that junk the caterpillar gets. No sooner do I read the title than five little hands go up in the air.

"Do all of y'all have questions?" I ask.

"I got that book at home," one boy says.

"Me, too," says another.

"Me-maw read it to me," says a little girl.

"Okay, lots of you have heard this one. Let's be quiet now, so everybody else can hear it, too." That seems to shut them up, at least temporarily.

But then, after only two pages, another boy raises his hand and without waiting to be called on says, "I caught me a callapitter. It was fuzzy and it felt funny when I touched it."

While he's yakking, a couple of boys start fighting. Their moms don't even pay attention. So I just continue on with the story. Next thing I know, one of those boys throws his tennis shoe at the other, only it misses and hits me right upside the head!

"Ow!" I yelp.

Then all hell breaks loose. Everybody is taking off their shoes and throwing them at each other and laughing like it's some kind of party.

Miss Patsy rushes in to save the day. "Children," she commands, and they all sit right down cross-legged on the rug. She takes the book from my hand and starts reading in this dramatic, dreamy voice, and the darn kids are transfixed.

I slink out to go finish shelving books, my head still stinging from that boy's shoe.

When I'm fixing to leave for the day, Miss Patsy comes over and says, "It'll get easier with the children. You just need to know how to hold their attention."

I nod, feeling embarrassed that things got so out of hand. The kids have been chatty and restless before, but it's never been this bad.

She hands me a copy of *Stallion of My Heart*. With a sly smile, she says, "I checked it out for you. If you're going to read it, may as well do it on your own time, though I'd prefer to see you reading something a little more challenging."

"Yes, ma'am. Thank you," I say, taking it from her. Then I head out back to get my bike. Not my best day at work.

I spy Surferboy playing basketball on the court behind the library with his cousin Junior. The other cousin, Billy Jo, is sitting up in their red pickup, wearing the Carolina Mudcats baseball cap that never seems to leave his head. He's blasting hip-hop so loud on the stereo the bass makes me woozy. While Junior is distracted with swiping his long, brown hair away from his eyes, Surferboy knocks the ball out of his hands and it flies my way. Next thing I know, he's running right straight towards me. I try to look busy unlocking my bike, make it seem like I wasn't just sitting there watching him.

"Hey," he says, picking up the ball.

"Hi," I reply, but then I hop on my bike and act like I'm busy closing up the lock.

He keeps looking at me.

Suddenly, I just can't handle the pressure. So I take off, riding for home.

"Hey!" he calls.

But now I feel like such a goon, rushing away like that, I just wave and keep on pedaling. This day is falling seriously flat. I'd best head home anyhow, see to it Dog's got his chores done.

I've lived in the same house my whole life—a little yellow square with one bathroom and two bedrooms, which, as you might have guessed, is totally insufficient. Can you imagine a fifteen-year-old girl having to share her bedroom with her twelve-year-old brother? It's downright embarrassing. I've been trying to convince Mama to let Dog move into the living room or down to the storm cellar. But as of yet, I'm having no luck. She's sure if he was in the living room he'd never cut off the television; and the cellar, well, if I were to be truthful, it ain't exactly what you'd call habitable. But with a little work . . .

I come in to find my brother kicked back on the couch looking at TV.

"Have you done your chores?" I ask him.

He grunts in response.

"Dog, I asked you a question."

"She ain't back yet," he replies.

"I refuse to take any heat for you on this." I turn the television off and stand right in front of it.

"What in the hell is up your butt?" he yells.

"I don't feel like being in trouble—*again*—for not making sure you get your chores done. I just got home from breaking my back shelving books all afternoon, while you were off playing."

"Calm yourself, woman," he teases, "I'm on it," then saunters out of the room.

All I can say is, three more years then I am out of here. I don't know where I'll end up, but I do know this: college is my ticket to somewhere else. I've worked my butt off my whole life to see to it that I get to go. I'll be the first one in my family to do so. How we'll afford it is a question I ain't ready to tackle just yet. But I'll tell you, I sure as hell am not sticking around this crappy-ass town. Mama says the ocean will call me back, keep me from straying too far. I think she's crazy as a cuckoo bird.

She grew up on the northern coast of North Carolina, on the edge of an area called—I kid you not—the Great Dismal Swamp. Can you imagine? When she finished high school, she cut out like a light—went over to Cary, this little town over by Raleigh. She got herself a job waitressing. That's where she met my daddy. But Mama missed the ocean something fierce and Daddy wanted to be a fisherman. So they moved down south to the beach. Mama likes it better here than where she grew up. I ain't clear on why. But I've never been up there to the Great Dismal Swamp, never even met my own grandma. She and Mama had some kind of falling-out—I expect having something to do with my daddy. That was before I was even born.

I've never been anywhere, really. We had a vacation once, when I was a baby—went up to the Blue Ridge Mountains to see the fall foliage. Mama says it was right beautiful. I don't remember a thing. That was back when she and Daddy were still happy and all. I've seen mountains on the TV and in the movies, of course. But I can't imagine what it'd be like in person, having that big old mound of earth rising up in front of you. I guess some folks can't imagine what the ocean is like, and I've got that right here in my own backyard.

Towards the end of this school year, my English teacher, Mrs. Avery, put my name in for something called the Program for Promising High School Students, which is like a semester-long college experience for tenth-graders. It's up in the Blue Ridge Mountains. I'm real excited to have been nominated. Each school can only recommend one student. Then only fifty kids get to go, and that's from both of the Carolinas. They live up there in the dorms just like real undergraduates. I ain't getting my hopes up too high. Nobody from our school has ever been selected to go. I keep wishing this time it might be me. But even if I was lucky enough for that to happen, we couldn't never afford it. I filled in my part of the application anyhow and sent it along with Mrs. Avery's forms. I didn't bother telling Mama about it. I just stuck the parent-signature page at the bottom of a stack of papers from school she needed to sign on a night when she was particularly tired. She didn't even look at it. No matter, it ain't exactly likely that they'll choose me. I reckon I'll have to wait until after high school to get out of this town. Then my first stop will be them mountains. I'll go check out that fall foliage, maybe on my way to college, wherever that may be.

Life here is just too boring. Or, at least . . . it was.

2

Mama was off to her job early again this morning. I don't have to work today, and my two best friends are out of town. Stef is at sleepaway camp, where she spends nearly half the summer, and Joie is with her family in Florida, visiting their people down there. So, I'm going to lay down in my hammock with a big ol' glass of sweet tea and a romance novel and relax, try to keep my mind from replaying how lame I must have seemed running off from that cute guy behind the library yesterday. I can't quit ruminating on it.

I finished reading *Stallion of My Heart* late last night. In the summertime I generally like to read trashy books. You know the ones I mean, with the ladies with their big bosoms on the cover and the muscle guys tearing at their clothes. I never read that stuff during the year, but come summer, I can't help myself. For school I'm always having to get through the likes of *David Copperfield* or *Romeo and*

Juliet, books where the English is so thick you've got to go over every paragraph six times before you understand what it is they're aiming to say. By the time summer comes around, my brain needs a rest. So you can see how a steamy romance would hit the spot like a cool summer breeze.

Speaking of which, there ain't nary a draft in sight, and this humidity is curling up my hair something fierce. The bees are buzzing around my tea, and the mosquitoes are surely biting. So much for my long, lazy afternoon. I believe a storm may be headed this way—the air has that feeling of pressure to it. It's hotter than a fish in a fry pan. I'm going to go inside, see if I can't cool down a mite.

Just as I'm opening the screen door, I see a familiar red pickup drive by. It's them Channing boys. I watch a minute to see if they've got my surfer in there with them and wonder again what he must think after I took off like that yesterday. He doesn't notice me at first, but then he leans his head way out the window to turn and wave like he's glad to see me. Then I hear them Channings howling with laughter. It is damn near hellish living in the same town since the day you were born, where everybody knows your entire life story and remembers the time you peed your pants in kindergarten. Can't never get away from your past.

I've got the fridge door open to get some cool air, but what I really want is to climb on up inside it. I wonder what his name is—maybe Wade or Walker or Harrison. I bet it ain't so ordinary and plain as his kinfolk, John William (that's Junior) or William John (known as Billy Jo). Their truck was headed toward the beach. Maybe I'll slip on my suit and ride on down there for a swim. Nothing can cool you off when it's muggy like a dip in the chilly ocean waves.

There's a bunch of kids from school laying out for a tan as if the sun was shining right through them clouds, but I don't see no sign of Surferboy. I'd go on over and say hey to them, but they're just a bunch of rednecks that live out to the farms up the road, always looking for trouble—tipping cows and whatnot. You may think I'm country, but you ain't seen nothing till you met them farm folk. I'm talking country as a bowl of grits.

Oh Lord, I got a prickling on the back of my neck. Either somebody walked over my grave or else I'm being watched.

I turn to look and there he is, staring right at me from up by the snack shack. Some kind of crazy zingy feeling goes shooting right on up my chest. I should have brung my inhaler—all the sudden my breathing is clunky. Hell 'n' high water, he's headed this way. And he's got that big ol' smile plastered on his face like I'm his long-lost best friend. And I haven't a clue what his long-lost best friend would say. I drop my bike down in the sand beside me.

"Hey," he says, just like last time.

Ah, hell. "Hey," I reply, promising myself that no matter what happens I will not run off like a baby.

"We met behind the library," he says.

"I remember you," I say, all shy-like. "I'm Savannah, you know, as in Georgia." Hells bells, I should have kept my mouth shut.

But he smiles at me with those sparkly sea-green eyes. "Jackson," he says, "as in Mississippi."

I'm fixing to fall out just turning that name over in my mouth. I knew he weren't no John or William. And that's when it happens.

I feel my chest cave in, and all the sudden I can't get no air. Mama's going to kill me for forgetting my inhaler. My eyes seem to pop right out of my head. I reckon I must look like the devil's own bride.

"Sump'n wrong?" he asks as I gasp and cough. I know my face is turning red.

"Asthma," I croak, feeling desperate and dumb as a dishrag, both.

"You got one of them inhalers or something?" he asks, looking concerned.

"At home," I manage to say.

He pulls up my bike and sets me on the seat, then straddles it in front of me. Without so much as a look back to his cousins, he rides me straight on home to my house, me sitting sidesaddle on the banana seat, my hand grabbing hold of his shirt to keep from falling. Even in my terrified state of oxygenless existence, I can't help but enjoy the warmth of his body so near to mine. I guess it's a good thing he drove by with his cousins earlier, 'cause I ain't exactly in a state to give directions.

He follows me inside, and I take a couple of hits off my inhaler. "Sorry about that. It don't happen too often," I lie, feeling like God's own fool.

"Ain't your fault," he says. Now ain't that a gentleman?

"Naw, my daddy's more like," slips out of my mouth before I can stop it.

"How you reckon?" he asks.

Blushing, I wave off his question. "Sorry you had to carry me home. I mean, thank you." It suddenly dawns on me how much trouble I'll be in if Mama comes back and finds me there with a guy all by myself.

I ain't technically allowed to have boys over unsupervised.

He seems to catch my brain wave, 'cause he says, "I guess I best be going."

But I so do not want him to leave. "I could give you a ride back down," I offer, grinning ear to ear. "I owe you one."

He laughs. It's a magical sound—richer than I would've imagined. "A'ight then, but I get the seat this time," he warns.

And then, as it often does right after an asthma attack, that funny feeling comes over me where I suddenly somehow know what's heading down the pipe. It's like when you've been trying real hard to remember something, and as soon as you quit, bam! There it is. This time what pops into my head is a big old feeling of heartache. But I set it aside and ride that grown boy right on down to the beach, him hanging onto the pockets of my shorts, as I stand in front of him, pedaling.

"Where'd you get off to?" Billy Jo asks soon as we hit the sand. "We been looking all over for you."

"I guess I better go," he says quietly, looking away.

"Thanks again," I say.

The Channings hoot and holler as if we've just been rolling around in the hay. And before Jackson and I can exchange so much as one more word, they haul him off, and I'm left there feeling as disappointed as a raccoon after the trash truck comes.

3

"Savannah, what are you carrying on about?" Mama asks me one afternoon as I'm blessing out my brother for leaving his crap all across my bed.

"Mama, I can't take no more of this. I'm near 'bout ready to kill him," I say, trying to keep myself from tearing Dog's head off. It's bad enough I've got to live with NASCAR posters plastered across his side of the room, but when there's baseball bats and gloves and balls and dirty dishes all over the floor and his stinky clothes and comic books strewn across my bed, I have got to draw the line.

She takes one look at our room and says, "Young man, you best clean up this mess directly or you gonn' be outside cutting me a switch."

Now Dog and I both know perfectly well that's an empty threat. Mama ain't never used a switch on neither one of us. She may talk big, but she don't hit.

So Dog says, "I'm heading out with Dave to play some ball."

"Indeed you are not," she replies, giving him that look that'll set your teeth on edge.

I can see the exact moment when he caves. "Fine, but Vannah better help."

"Don't one piece of that mess belong to me," I start in, but Mama cuts me off.

"Hush your mouth," she says, shooing me out of the room. I leave, but I can hear her talking to Dog all civil, telling him how she needs him to straighten up right quick, and she ain't just meaning his things.

I ambush her as soon as she steps out to the living room. "Please let him move in here. I am too old to be sharing—"

She interrupts me. "You are wearing on my last nerve, girl. I told you it ain't gonn' happen. You think I want his mess all over the house? It's bad enough when it's confined to y'all's room."

I know I'm pushing my luck, but I can't stop myself. "Maybe we could get some church folk over here to help build us on an extra room or fix up the cellar."

"I am warning you, I can't think no more about this today," she says, sounding evil as a goat.

I know when to leave well enough alone, so I head outside to get out of her hair before she blows her top. I believe I'll take myself a walk along the railroad tracks. It ain't like I'm planning on going over to the Channings' place. I ain't that crazy. But you never know who you might could meet when you're out walking.

Before I know it, I find myself just up the hill from the Channings'.

I haven't met a soul along the way, and the house looks still. I reckon nobody else is crazy enough to go out walking when it's 95 degrees and humid as all get out. I choose me a spot in the tall, itchy grass to sit down and see if I can't catch sight of Jackson. A fierce but silent trill runs right up my chest at the thought of that name. They could have gone out fishing first thing this morning for all I know. No matter. Long as I don't got to be putting in my hours at the library or doing chores at home, I can spend my time however I like.

To be perfectly honest, during the school year, I study as if my life depended upon it, which, if you ask Mama, it very well may. She's been on me since day one about getting good grades so I don't end up working slave-wage jobs like her. I reckon all that work has paid off, though. I'm at the very top of my class, and I ain't just bragging on myself neither.

Ever since I can remember, Mama has given me some kind of workbook to keep up my skills during the summer. They've got titles like *Get Ready for Kindergarten*, or *Math Every Sixth Grader Should Know*, or in this year's case *Preparing for the SAT*. Some kids come home from school on the last day and get a swimsuit or maybe a new pair of skates for good report cards, something to encourage them to enjoy their summer. Not me, a workbook is my reward for a year of hard work. She gave up on Dog even opening his, somewhere around the first grade. Every year, I've got mine finished by the time school starts back. It may sound geeky, but I like being able to make her proud. All my brother has to do to please her is stay out of trouble.

Anyhow, since it's only the beginning of summer and I don't

have to be at work until four, I'm going to just sit here and watch the daggum grass grow.

Holy Mother of God! There's Jackson. He's heading up to the tracks by himself, and here I am spying on their house plain as day. I hadn't thought about the likelihood of having to explain myself. It ain't even like I'm laying out at the beach or somewhere normal. I'm hiding in the grass right out by their place. My face is burning up. I can't think what to do.

He's got headphones in his ears, the music turned up so loud I can hear it all the way over to here. Maybe he won't notice me. Okay, the grass ain't that tall. But then all the sudden I get a feeling that something just ain't right. I haven't a clue what it's about. I just feel edgy is all. I'm thinking real hard on what it might could mean, when, holy swear word, there is an honest-to-God train coming up behind him. I swear there ain't been a train on these tracks my entire life, and there is one racing up behind him faster than hell on wheels.

"Jackson! Jackson!" I yell, imagining that train plowing into him and his body flying off the tracks in a million bits. But he ain't hearing me with them headphones plugged in. I've got no choice but to hurl myself at him like a crazy person. I run as fast as I can and literally throw myself at him, knocking him down to the grass as the three-car train whistles on by.

You can see he's all confused and trying to make sense of what just happened. I can't speak at all, I'm so choked up by the whole thing. And he's sitting there looking at me like I'm Jesus himself.

"You saved my life," he says all addled-like.

I shrug—what else could I have done? "I reckon I owed you one," I say, finding my voice.

And then, glory hallelujah, that smile comes over his face that like to set me on fire.

"Sump'n tells me I may as well make a point of knowing you, Savannah as in Georgia," he says, which sends a shiver right up my spine.

"I hurt you a-tall?" I ask, noting how he's rubbing his neck.

He looks off after the train. "Not so bad as that woulda. I thought there weren't no trains on these tracks."

"There ain't."

"How'd you get here, anyways?" he asks.

Ruther than get into all the specifics of what I was doing sitting out in the grass practically stalking him, I just say, "I had a feeling is all."

"That I was about to get run down by a train that ain't s'posed to exist?" he asks.

I shake my head, not sure how to explain myself.

"You had a feeling, huh?" he says, staring at me. "I had a sense there was sump'n unusual about you."

I like to fall out the way he's looking at me. Is it possible he may actually think I'm cute? Is it too much to hope for? I mean, I know I ain't ugly or nothing, but I ain't exactly model material neither. I guess most folks would call me about average—that goes for my weight, my height, and pretty much everything else—just sort of plain, although I have been told my eyes are the color of cornflowers. (Does it count if my own mama said it?)

Junior and Billy Jo stroll out of the house, and I fear our moment has ended.

But Jackson goes, "Shh. Let's get outta here," and points at his kin as if to tell me he doesn't want them to see us. We creep over into the bushes on the far side of the tracks, then take off running.

I don't know if it's the high from saving Jackson like that, the nearness we came to seeing heaven's gates, or just being so close to the guy I've been crushing on that makes me so giddy, but before I know what I'm doing I find myself squealing like a toddler while we run. Now I am just as embarrassed as a pig at a picking (naked as a jaybird and a roasting spit up his backside). Jackson busts up laughing, not like he's funning me or nothing, just like he understands how durn-all happy I am. He takes my hand and tears on down the hill toward the beach, running so fast I'm all but flying.

Why is it whenever you find everything feeling right, it's all the time got to go and turn wrong? Soon as we hit the sand, Dog starts to yelling at Jackson, "You best watch out for her, dude. She's a handful! She'll wear you out!" He's playing baseball with Dave and some other kids. And now they've all turned to look at me.

"Shut up!" I call. Damn, my brother has got to be the most annoying human being on the face of this earth.

"You want me to tell Mama you got a boyfriend?"

I'm about ready to take that baseball bat out of his hands and knock him to kingdom come, when Jackson pipes up. "Go on and play ball. I suggest you leave her 'lone." And you can hear in his voice he means it. Ain't nobody ever looked out for me like that.

"Act like you got some raising!" I add to Dog.

"Whatchoo gonn' do 'bout it?" Dog insists on being his sorry self. That boy ain't got a lick of sense.

Jackson jumps like he's going to get him, then laughs when Dog turns tail. As we walk on, Jackson says all quietlike, "You got a boyfriend, huh?" And he's smiling at me from here to tomorrow.

The red rises right up my cheeks. "He don't know nothing," I say, not wanting Jackson to think I'm presuming anything. I haven't had a serious boyfriend yet. I mean, I've messed around some and there were guys I liked and all. But they don't count for real. That was just kid stuff.

"Come on," he says, taking my hand again and heading down the beach away from where everybody lays out.

We walk till we find a spot where there ain't so many folks all over and sit down in the sand to watch the surf with its bubbling white foam.

I can see Jackson drifting off in his thoughts, like something's on his mind. I ain't sure what to say really, but I know I want to bring him back here with me. "Where you from?" I finally get up the nerve to ask after practicing it in my head sixteen times.

"Greenville," he says.

"How come I ain't seen you here before this summer?" I wonder out loud, seeing as Greenville ain't all that far off.

He's quiet awhile, then he says, "I always helped my daddy in the summer, buildin' cabinets. We didn't have time to kick back at the beach like Junior and Billy Jo."

"Why'd you get to come out this year?" I ask.

He shrugs. "My dad passed on in April, had himself a heart

attack." Looking out to the sea, he says, "Guess my ma thought it'd be good for me, you know, get away from everything for a spell. So she sent me to his brother's family for the summer."

"I'm sorry," I say, my stomach twisting up like the tornado I was named after. "What you hope to do come fall?"

He looks right straight at me and smiles. "Maybe I'll find me a reason to stick around here awhile." Honest to God. Can you believe it?

"I hope so," I say.

And then, as if God is sitting up in heaven watching us, thinking we need a cooling down, the tide comes and chases us up the beach. By the time we settle back in the sand, the mood has shifted.

"Thought I might like to try paintin' houses," he says, but there's a look in his eye tells me something ain't right.

"Houses? What you want to do that for?"

He turns away and looks out to the sea as if he might find my answer there. "Sump'n wrong with paintin' houses?"

"Hell no," I say. "I just got an inkling of a feeling that that ain't all there is to it."

"You got a feeling, huh? There ain't no shark coming after me, is there?"

I swat him on the arm for that one. "Be serious!"

But then his face turns all still and he goes, "Naw, you're right. I cain't lie. What I really want to do is paint for real, you know, like pitures. I ain't talking about doing portraits for rich folk—more like, you know, putting onto the canvas sump'n I see in my head, sump'n I cain't even describe into words, but give me a brush and I sure as hell can show you. I want to travel the world and put what I see into my pitures." Then he blushes like he's all embarrassed for being honest. And if that don't give me the goosiest goose bumps you ever did see!

"I want to travel, too," I say. "First, I aim to see the Blue Ridge Mountains. But then I want to go on and check out the rest of the world. I'ma go to college and get me a real good job, maybe like a journalist or a writer of stories of far-off lands, something where your work pays you to go all over."

Right then his nasty old cousins come upon us. "Jackson, what are you doing with a lowly townie when just across them rocks is a beach full of city girls?" Billy Jo calls. "Y'all fixing to go at it?"

"Jailbait!" Junior adds, laughing.

Jackson turns three shades of red and stands to leave.

I'm sitting here feeling all desperate, wanting to think up something, anything that would cause him to want to see me again. But I can't drum up a durn thing.

Then he turns to me and smiles as big as that ocean and says, "I'll call you," right there in front of them cousins, which of course just makes them hoot even louder. But he don't seem to care.

"My last name's Brown!" I call after him, seeing as I didn't get a chance to give him my number. At least now he can look it up in the phone book.

I head home to get my bike, wishing Stef wasn't off at that dumb camp of hers. It lasts till the middle of July. I need someone who's more experienced with guys to talk to about Jackson. I know she'd tell me not to worry about his kin and their ugly teasing. She'd say he's for sure into me and all. But I wish I could hear it from her directly.

As I ride my bicycle through town, I pass by the junior college, then loop back around to it. After stowing my bike in the rack, I peek into some of the classrooms. Somewhere in there is the Living Through Literature program. It's this real cool (okay maybe dorky, but still) camp type of thing where you read classic books and learn about the authors and the eras when they wrote their stories. I believe they put on some plays, too. You even get school credit for it. My guidance counselor called me into her office at the end of the year to tell me about it, since I had the highest grade in my English class and Mrs. Avery recommended me.

Once the counselor mentioned there wasn't any financial aid available, I just acted like I thought it was dumb. I didn't even bother telling Mama about it. There ain't a chance in hell of us being able to afford such a thing, and I didn't want to make her feel bad.

I wander around the campus, imagining what it'll be like to be in college someday—not at this dinky little school, I hope. If I'm lucky, it'll be somewhere far off.

I peek at the labels on all the classroom doors until I find the Living Through Literature group. I slip into the back of the auditorium to watch. There's about twenty kids down in front. I recognize a few from school, and they ain't even all that smart. It sure looks like they're having fun. One of the teachers is talking, and the kids are laughing. It don't make no never mind.

"Can I help you?" asks one of the other teachers, who's standing near the back.

Turning red, I slide back out the door right quick. I best get to work anyhow, before I get myself fired. Even the monotony of shelving books won't be able to take the shine off a day at the beach with Jackson Channing.

4

I come in for supper humming a little tune without even realizing I'm doing it till Mama says, "What's up with you?"

"What?" I ask, quitting my humming. I don't want her knowing about Jackson yet. Don't want her fretting and imposing rules, tethering the dream before it has a chance to fly.

But you know I can't get that lucky. In walks Dog with a big ol' grin on his sorry face. "Hey there, Miss Uppity Channing." That's the best he could come up with? I reckon he's aiming to impress me with his resourcefulness in finding out who Jackson is.

"Hello to you, *Mrs.* Davis Wilson." I got him good with that one. If there's anyone on this earth with a bad case of that homophobia, it's Dog.

"Shut your face, Vannah!" he shouts.

"Shut yours, you cow!" I retort.

Next thing I know, he's walloping me on the back of my head.

Then I've got a hank of his hair and I'm pulling on it, when Mama yells, "That's it! Both of y'all are on punishment tonight," which sucks, except for the fact that it's caused Mama to forget all about my humming.

Dog starts to whining. But I don't care none. I ain't a big TV person anyhow, and with Stef at camp, where no phone calls are allowed, and Joie off in Florida busy with her family (who are too stingy to let her make long-distance calls), I hadn't any plans to be on the phone this evening. I've got a new romance to read—*The Flower and the Flame*—and my journal to write in. So I'm happy. Poor Dog can't occupy himself for even a minute.

His face is all splotchy. "She provoked me on purpose!"

"Seems to me you the one started the whole thing," Mama says. "Now go on to your room till supper's ready. I don't want to hear another word outta you."

I silently set the table to get back into Mama's good graces, hoping she won't ask me nothing.

"You remembering 'bout the church picnic on Sundy evenin'?"

"Yes, ma'am."

"You gonn' fix the potata salad for me so it's ready when I get home from work, right?"

"Yes, ma'am." I ain't taking no chances of stirring up the waters tonight. Besides, the Channings go to our church, so Jackson's liable to be at the picnic, too.

Would you believe, just as I'm thinking that, the phone rings? My heart misses a beat. But I'm sure it won't be him.

Then I hear Mama say, "No, she can't come to the phone tonight.

She's on punishment." And damn, but my cheeks go red. "Who is this?"

I focus on going about my business as if it ain't nothing, so Mama won't notice how crazy I'm going inside, as she finishes up the call.

Here she comes looking at me all suspicious.

"Who was that?" I ask, trying to sound like I don't even care.

"Some young man. Something about a poll they're doing, asking young people questions about the state of the world." She's eyeballing me something fierce now, waiting to see if I'll crack. I just shrug my shoulders and head over to the counter to work on the salad. I can't help but smile when I think of him coming up with that hogwash.

"Anybody new around town this summer?" Mama asks.

"How should I know? Do I look like the welcome wagon?" Sweat starts to bead up on my forehead. I just wipe it on the back of my hand and keep chopping the vegetables.

Lucky for me, Mama notices the greens are burning, and that takes her mind off the mystery caller.

Soon as she leaves for the Family Dollar the next morning, the telephone rings.

I race into the kitchen and pick it up. "Hello," I say. Dog's still laying up in the bed—lazy-ass.

"You off punishment already?" Jackson laughs.

I catch my breath and feel like a whole cage full of butterflies have been let go and are flying up from my stomach to my chest.

"That was a good one—that survey thing." I can feel him smiling through the phone.

Then his voice gets kind of scratchy, and he says all seriouslike, "Meet me at the beach?"

I start to fanning myself with my hand. "When?"

"Soon as you can get there."

"Ten minutes," I tell him, then rush off to the bathroom to shave my legs and brush my teeth. I go as fast as I can, then ride my bike like I'm fleeing from an atomic bomb. But still, when I get there, I see him sitting on the sand like he's been waiting on me all day.

"Hey, Savannah," he says, and his voice sounds grown and smooth.

"Hey," I say back.

Then we just stand there, not knowing what to do. There ain't hardly nobody on the beach, except some fishermen. And we just look at each other till we both bust out laughing.

Then he takes me by the hand and we walk up the coastline with no destination. We climb across the rocks to where the sand turns near white and the beach fills up with city folk and fancy vacation homes. We keep on, slow but steady, chitchatting about seashells and folks we pass along the way.

"You got any brothers or sisters?" I ask him.

"Two brothers. Carter's fifteen and Tyler's fourteen."

I wonder if that makes me seem young to him. Then I suddenly realize he probably doesn't even know my age. "You get along with 'em?" I ask.

He shrugs. "I reckon they're closer to each other." Then he gets that far-off look in his eyes and starts to staring out to sea.

I scrounge up my nerve and ask him, "Whatcha thinking 'bout?"

"Wondering what's out there for me."

"Something real special," I tell him.

"You got a feeling on that?" he asks.

Blushing, I shake my head. "I just sense you're different is all."

"Different?" he asks me. "How you reckon?"

I turn to the ocean, try to find my answer out that way. "I don't know." I shrug, wanting to be truthful, yet fearing it at the same time. "You seem . . . real." I turn back towards him. "Folks are always trying so hard to seem this way or that way or not seem some way or the other. I like how you told me about your dream of painting and how you said you'd call me in front of your kin when they was teasing us, and then you were true to your word and called. You just seem . . . trustworthy, like you're who you say you are . . . just you."

He shrugs, looking out at the waves again. "Got no one else to be."

"It's kinda funny," I say, thinking aloud, "how that one simple thing is so hard for most folk."

"What?" he asks.

"Just being theirselves."

He looks at me all serious, his eyes deep and intense. And I get to thinking maybe he's going to kiss me right there. Then a great big smile breaks over his face like the wave crashing on the shore and he says, "Let's go swimming." And next thing I know he's splashing into the water, tugging me along with him, my shorts and T-shirt still on top of my swimsuit. I swear this guy is crazy. And damn, but I'm loving every minute.

"Our church is having a cookout Sunday evening," I tell him, as I dip my hair back in the water to get it out of my face. "You think you might could go? It's the same one your kin go to."

"I'll check with my aunt. You gonn' be there?" he asks.

My smile is near about breaking my face in two. I nod.

"We'll see what we can do then." He grins and pulls me under the next wave.

Later, on my way to work, I swing by the junior college again, peek in on that camp. I ease into the back of the darkened auditorium real quiet this time, then creep into a chair, slunk down real low so nobody'll notice.

The kids and teachers are sitting in a big circle up on the bright stage talking. I can't hear, so I move closer, staying down. It's *Jane Eyre* they're discussing. I read that book last year. I liked that the romance had a happy ending. But it killed me how long it took them to get there. I never understood how Jane could keep from getting together with Mr. Rochester all that time. I mean, I know he was her boss and well, married to a crazy woman and all. But in my opinion, love just isn't something that can be overcome.

"In the eighteen eighties," the teacher is saying, "when Miss Brontë wrote the novel, women were expected to tend to the home. What free time they had was to be spent on productive pastimes such as knitting, or those that entertained, like piano playing. Writing was considered men's work, which is why the book was originally published under a pseudonym."

I am certainly glad not to have lived at that time. I couldn't stand tending to the house all day, not being allowed to follow my own dreams just 'cause I was a girl.

"When it was discovered that a woman had written the novel, critics thought it immoral that she could express such passion," the teacher says.

Well, I never! I say good for her and good riddance!

I'm itching to stay and hear more about what it was like back then, but I really ought to get to work.

When I arrive at the library, I head straight into the stacks to find a copy of *Jane Eyre*. I skip around in it, going back over the parts I liked best. I'm rereading the one where Jane finds out that her true love's crazy wife, who was locked up in the attic, set the house on fire, killing herself and blinding the dude Jane loves, when Miss Patsy clears her throat rather loudly, her eyebrows raised.

"Sorry," I murmur, setting the book aside for later and getting to work. It's near to closing time, and I've got loads of books to put up. I'm rushing around when Dog and Dave stroll in.

"Vannah," my brother calls out loud, as if he were on the playground.

"Shh!" I warn.

He rolls his eyes. "Ain't nobody in here," he says, as Dave giggles.

"Shh!" Miss Patsy holds her finger up over her lips.

"Oh, fine," Dog says. They come over to me. "Tell Mama I'll be in late tonight. Me and Dave are eating over with some friends."

"Hey, Dave," I say. "What friends, Dog?" Mama's words come out of my mouth.

"Just some kids from school," he replies. "Quit giving me the third degree."

"Come on, Dave," I say, knowing he's the weaker link. "Whose house you gonn' be at, in case Mama or Gina want to call?"

"Y'all don't know him," Dave says quietly.

"Just tell her I'll be back late," Dog insists.

"Be home by dark!" I call after them as they bolt.

"Shh!" Miss Patsy hisses.

After work, Mama comes into my room, where I'm writing in my journal, and starts in to yelling at me for not knowing whose house Dog and Dave are at. How am I supposed to keep track of every one of their friends, I ask you? Oh well, I reckon she's just tired and not in the mood to worry over them. I suppose it's easier to take it out on me.

5

I'm laying up in the hammock a couple days later, listening to music and daydreaming about Jackson, when I suddenly get a creeping feeling I done forgot something important. It's that sense that overtakes you right quick and you know it ain't like you forgot your flip-flops at the beach, more like you're about to meet up with some serious trouble. I sit up and try to figure out what day we're on when it suddenly hits me—today's Sunday. Holy you-know-what, Mama's going to be home from work in fifteen minutes, and I haven't even started to boil the potatoes for the salad.

Damn! Where is my brain lately? I better shape up or Mama is sure to notice that my thoughts are elsewhere. Lord, there ain't no way I can get this salad fixed before she gets home. She's going to be sopping mad.

I'm boiling the water and scrubbing the potatoes when Dog wanders in and says, "Vannah, fix me a sandwich. I'm damn near starved."

Bless his heart but he pushed me at the wrong time. "Fix your own damn food, you heifer! The church cookout ain't but a half hour from now." I am running around the kitchen gathering the ingredients for the salad, but let's face it, ain't nothing going to make those potatoes boil any faster.

"Who peed in your cornflakes this morning?" he asks.

"I'ma tan your hide if you don't get outta here!" Course it's me I'm mad at, but I'm so riled up now, knowing how p.o.'d Mama's going to be, I can't seem to stop myself. "Either start chopping or get out, one," I say.

"You on the rag or something?" he says as he struts out of the room and flicks on the TV.

That boy is so crass. Course it ain't never him that's expected to fix the damn salad or help with supper or anything else. Mama always used to say it was 'cause he was too little. But the boy is twelve years old! I've been helping since I was near about six. What, does she reckon he'll run off like our daddy if she puts him to work around the house?

I'm just hoping Mama doesn't restrict me from the picnic as my punishment. I believe Jackson may show up, and I'm just itching to see him. I looked for him at the beach the last few days, but he hasn't been there, and he hasn't called either. I already picked out a real cute sundress to wear that looks right pretty on me.

I've got everything all mixed up in the bowl, just waiting on the potatoes to get tender, when the phone rings. "You got the salad ready to go?" Mama asks.

I ponder on that one a half second. If she's calling me, she's likely still at the store, seeing as she still has not given in to getting us a cell phone. And if she hasn't left yet, I can surely get it ready by the time she gets home. "Yes, ma'am."

"Good girl. I know I can always count on you, baby."

Is she testing me?

"I'm afraid I'ma have to be late to the supper. Jolene ain't here yet, and Sonny won't let me go till she gets here. Y'all go on down to the picnic, and I'll meet you there directly."

My mind goes straight to how awful I'm going to look after walking two miles in the humidity. As if it ain't cruel enough that Dog got Mama's thick, bouncy hair and I got stuck with the thin, limp kind, when it's humid out, my dirty-blond locks sag like a wet mutt. "Dog ain't gonn' like having to walk," I say.

"Y'all can ride bikes if you'd ruther."

"How'm I gonn' tote the salad?" I ask.

"Ride my bike," she offers. "I got the basket on the front."

Great. Now I get to arrive looking like that old witch in *The Wizard of Oz*.

Once we get there, I try to fluff up my hair, but the humidity is thick and my hair is plastered right to my head. Dog runs off to find Dave without so much as a "see ya later" to me. I set the potato salad down on one of the long tables next to a whole mess of macaroni salads, slaw, cooked greens, and fried okra. The next table over makes my mouth water with its hush puppies and corn sticks, double-crisp battered fries and biscuits. I ain't as fired up about the next one with the Brunswick stew (looks like somebody's been sick in the pot) and beef tips on rice (otherwise known as shit on a shingle, pardon my French) and fried catfish (them things got whiskers, for heavens sakes!). But I must admit the barbecue looks and smells mighty good. Our preacher is hands down the best barbecuer in the county. The dessert table is full to the brim with brownies, cookies, banana pudding with vanilla wafers, red velvet cake, key lime pie, strawberry shortcake, watermelon slices (with a salt shaker on hand for those who like it that way), peach cobbler with a big ol' tub of Cool Whip, and three whole trays of Dunkin' Donuts.

"Is that Savannah Brown?" ol' Miss Caroline Watson asks. She's older than dirt and just as much in everybody's business as the day she was born. I try not to look at the long white hairs hanging off her chin. Mama says if you focus on that type of thing you'll be sure to get it yourself someday. "Where's your mama at, honeychile? I ain't seen her at church for nary a—"

"I hear you got another birthday coming up, Miss Caroline," I say, just to get her off the topic of Mama not being much of a churchgoer.

"The good Lord willing and the creek don't rise," she says.

Good night, I'm thinking, rolling my eyes in my mind. "I believe I see some of my friends over yonder. I'll speak with you later on, ma'am," I say, trying my best to be polite. I go over and chat with some kids from bible group. Truth be told I ain't been in a couple years. But I still see them at school and so forth.

Now here's something I hadn't figured on. Mama's headed straight for me from one direction. And here comes Jackson smiling at me from the other. All I want is to go sit together on a blanket under a tree and just stare back into his eyes. But Mama's nearly here, and I ain't ready for them to meet up.

The Lord must be on my side suddenly, because Miss Caroline and her troop of in-everybody's-business do-gooders waylay Mama, giving me just enough time to greet Jackson and disappear with him before she even knows I'm gone.

"I was hoping I'd see you here tonight," I say once we've found a quiet spot behind a tree.

"You look right beautiful, Savannah," he says, causing me to blush something fierce. *Beautiful!*

"Where you been lately?" I ask, hoping I don't seem too pushy.

"Just dealing with some problems back home," he says. "But I've been thinking about you."

My cheeks burn. "Anybody sees us behind this tree, the whole church'll be talking."

"Let 'em talk." His smile is so big I feel like I could just crawl right on up inside it. "What you worried about?" he asks all tender, brushing the back of his finger along my face. Whoo boy, I set to quivering, fearing my knees may buckle.

"If Mama finds out—" I say, but then I stop, 'cause I ain't sure what it is exactly we've got going here, and I don't want to make a fool of myself by presuming.

He steps closer to me. And next thing I know, his warm, soft lips are touching mine. He pulls away and smiles down at me, and honest to God I am swooning. "Now that's sump'n to talk about," he whispers.

Much as I wish we could just stay here kissing all evening, I keep thinking about Dog or Mama coming around the side of the tree. And if she finds out I'm kissing a grown boy she ain't never met at the church picnic, she's gonn' pitch a hissy fit with a tail on it. "Maybe we should get some supper," I suggest.

"Mm," he says, staring at me all dreamy-eyed.

"Jackson, you gotta quit looking at me like that," I say, even though I'm squealing with joy inside.

"Like what?" he asks.

"You know." Now I'm blushing but good. "Don't get me wrong. It ain't that I don't like it, but Mama's out there. She'll bust a gut, and it won't be from laughing."

"Your mama got sump'n against the Channings?" he asks.

"No. My mama's got something against her fifteen-year-old daughter kissing a guy she don't know, with the preacher barbecuing not ten yards away."

"You only fifteen?" he asks, looking all shocked.

Shoot. I stepped right into that one. "I'll be fifteen and a half next month."

Well something about that just tickles him, and he starts to laughing and won't stop.

"How old are *you*?" I ask, knowing by his muscular build there ain't no way he's even close to fifteen.

"Eighteen," he says.

"She sure ain't gonn' like that," I reply. "We just won't tell her nothing for now."

"Can I at least hold your hand?" he asks, looking like a puppy.

Damn, do I want to say yes, but I set him straight anyhow. "Hell no. Soon as she knows about you, she'll be monitoring my every move. You can say good-bye to me having any free time. She'll have enough chores to keep me busy the rest of the summer."

Now he looks all pouty. "I thought you were looking forward to seeing me tonight."

"I was and I am. We just got to play it cool, that's all."

We head back to the tables and start to fill our plates.

"There you are, baby," Mama says, as she and Gina walk up to us. "I been looking all over for you."

"I've been right here," I say too quickly.

The two of them are chowing down on barbecue. Gina's drab-colored hair is all frizzy; I reckon the humidity ain't helping her out none, either.

"Who's your friend?" Mama asks.

Gina elbows her and giggles. She's got on a low-cut coral top and takes a second to adjust it. "Yes, I'd like to meet him," she says, wiping her hand on her pants.

My heart's thundering like a serious storm. "Who?" I say, looking about like I don't know who's standing right beside me. Mama gives me the hairy eyeball. "Oh, him. His name's uh, uh Jackson, I believe. He's kin to the Channings."

"That right?" Mama asks, holding out her hand to Jackson.

"Nice to meet you," he says. "Which one of these delicious dishes did you make, ma'am?"

Eyeing him but good, Mama says, "Savannah made the potata salad."

"Well, I'll have to try me some of that," he says, spooning an obscene amount of it onto his plate. Damn, I must have laid it on too thick—he's nervous.

"Where'd y'all meet?" Mama asks, trying to sound casual, but looking suspicious.

"At the beach," I say.

Except at the very same second, Jackson says, "At the library."

Of course both statements are true, but it don't look good. I slap my forehead. "How could I forget, first at the library—just for a minute or two, then at the beach, with his cousins," I add.

"You live around here, or you just visiting?" Gina asks, mashing down her hair.

"It ain't clear yet," Jackson says. "I'll be here through the summer for sure, then we'll see." And damn but he looks right at me! Smiling!

The jig is up. If Mama hadn't figured it out before, she most certainly has got it now. Gina's elbowing her in the gut. Mama's slapping away Gina's arm and glaring at me like she wants to know what all is going on.

And then, as if the devil was orchestrating the whole night, Miss Nosy-Face Caroline Watson waddles over and says, "Porsha,"—there was a Porsche commercial on the radio when Mama was born, but my grandma didn't know how to spell—"was that your young'un I saw over behind the trees earlier?" She's raising up her nasty, whiskery eyebrows at me. "I didn't realize she'd grown big enough for courtin'."

Gina gasps and starts laughing. Mama looks none too happy.

My face is burning red. Old gossip. I've got half a mind to tell that ol' biddy what I think of her. But suddenly I'm gasping for air.

"Thank you, Miss Caroline. I can take it from here." Mama turns her back on the woman, which I'm glad to see. "Savannah, where is your inhaler at?"

But everything's closing up inside and I can't focus on remembering what I did with my inhaler. I can't remember if I brung it along or not or where I last saw it or nothing. Before Mama can say a word against it, Jackson picks me up and carries me to the parking lot, with Mama tagging along behind.

Dog and Dave run up. "She okay?" my brother asks.

"She will be," Mama reassures.

Gina's got all our plates towering in her hands. "I'll keep Dog," she calls out. "Y'all go on!"

Waving to Gina, Mama yells to Jackson, "Check her pockets!" And I can feel his hands moving across my thighs, which only makes my breathing worse. He doesn't find what he's looking for, and he just keeps tearing across the lot. And to my surprise I find myself in the back of Mama's car, Jackson beside me, Mama up in front, and me wheezing like a geezer.

"Ma'am, you best step on it, she don't look too good." Mama screeches out of the parking lot and drives toward the hospital. "Ain't you headed the wrong way?" Jackson asks, looking all worried.

Mama pulls the car over to the side of the road. "You don't need to come along. It's too late to go home for the inhaler. I'ma have to carry her down to Mercy Hospital. Your folks'll be worried. You best go on home or back to the cookout, one. Thank you for your help."

I can feel Jackson hesitating and much as I wish he'd stay beside me, I wish even more he'd hurry up and go 'cause I do not like the way I'm feeling and I just want somebody to fix it right quick.

"Drive," he says. "I ain't leaving her like this."

Mama puts the car in gear and says, "Just met at the library, huh?"

And I am a stuck duck in a dry pond.

6

I'm relieved to see the emergency room looks pretty quiet, just a couple of hoboes seeming drunk, a twenty-something young man with blood spilling down his head, and a stressed-out family with one baby asleep on the chair and another whimpering, holding her arm up against her chest. The nurse shows me in right away and sets me up with the nebulizer; that's this thingamabob that sends mist into my lungs along with medicine, oxygen, all that type of stuff. I can tell you it is one big relief to feel that mist coming in, 'cause I know it means I'm going to be breathing right before long. No sooner does my panic begin to subside than they're searching my arm for a vein to prick. That part I hate, when they stick that needle in there for the IV and then the steroids start to flow into me. Ugh, gives me a chill just thinking about it. It's supposed to take down the swelling in my lungs so I can breathe easier, which is a good thing, but it makes me feel ill when they do it. Mama usually holds my hand, but that just ain't enough.

She's got her notebook out, marking down everybody's names and what all they're putting into me. They told Jackson he'd have to stay out in the waiting room. I feel bad for him, sitting out there, wondering if I'm okay. I wish Mama had said he was my brother so he might could come in. Seems downright rude to leave him out there after he done come all this way. I look to the door as I'm thinking about him, and law! He's standing right at the window peeking in at me. I can't help but smile. Out the corner of my eye I see Mama watching me, noting my smile, and following my eyes to see what's cheered me up in this awful place.

Next thing I know, she's opening the door and bringing Jackson over beside me. There's some commotion with the nurses, but Mama takes care of it. And then Jackson is sitting by me, holding my hand, and I ain't never minded an IV stick less in my whole life. His hand is warm and rough and safe. And he's looking all worried about me. Ain't that just the sweetest?

The doctor comes in, a big heft of a man with a fuzzy beard and mustache but not much of anything up top. He says I'm going to have to stay the night so they can keep an eye on me. Damn. I'm feeling so much better. I'd ruther go on home with Mama and Jackson. Sleeping in the hospital sucks, what with noise bothering you and nurses waking you up to take your vitals all night long and the smell of ammonia and alcohol so strong it could blind a person. Mama knows how I hate it, and she starts in on the doctor, asking can't I just go and come back tomorrow? But old baldy shakes his head and says this here was a rough one and I best stay the night. I'm thinking he's just needing a few more coins in his purse. Mama's got me on a special insurance program with the state to help pay my medical bills, but I know it still worries her when we've got to stay over. I take her hand for a minute to let her know how sorry I am.

As the nurses are fixing to take me upstairs, Mama offers to call a cab for Jackson. He says he'd ruther stay awhile. But Mama gets stern with him.

"Young man, you have sure impressed me tonight, wanting to be here with Savannah through this, but it's time you go on home. Your kin are probably wondering about you, and they ain't gonn' be too chipper 'bout you spending the night with the likes of us. It's late. We're all tired. I suggest you make tracks." And I can hear in her voice how worn she is.

"Ms. Brown, I ain't trying to be rude or nothing. I can call my aunt and uncle and tell 'em where I'm at. But they don't decide who I spend my time with. She still don't look right. If it's all the same to you, I'd ruther stay awhile and see how she does."

Shew! Ain't he sweet? We hardly even known each other but a week or two, and here he goes making all this fuss! Mama must think we've been hiding this for months.

"Well it ain't all the same to me," she snaps. But I grab her hand and look at her with eyes that say *Please, Mama!* And she softens. The nurse starts to push my wheelchair out to the elevator and Mama doesn't object when Jackson follows. "How old are you anyhow?" she asks him once the elevator doors close.

"Eighteen, ma'am," he replies. I can't help but flinch as I wonder how she's going to react to that one.

She turns to face him. "Do you know how old she is?" she asks like I'm not even there.

"Yes, ma'am. She's fifteen going on fifteen and a half," he says with a smile.

Mama just shakes her head.

They get me all tucked into bed. Mama scribbles in her notebook and Jackson sits in a chair beside me, leaning over me like he's scared I'm going to die.

I lift the nebulizer mask off my face. "You don't gotta stay," I whisper, not wanting Mama to hear. "I'll be okay."

He shakes his head and takes my hand. "You want me to go?" he whispers back.

Now I'm shaking my head. I just don't want him to feel obliged is all. And much as I'd like to hang out and talk with him, I feel myself getting so sleepy I can't keep my eyes open, and I know I'm drifting off.

I wake sometime later. The lights are dim and the TV's on low. Mama and Jackson are sitting in chairs on opposite sides of the bed, staring up at the screen, talking at each other without looking.

"Alls I'm saying is you best not break her heart."

"Why would I do that?"

Ppphhh, Mama blows through her lips. "She told you about her asthma before?"

"She said it don't happen too often."

"That's a bald-face lie. Trying not to run you off, I reckon."

And I'm betting Jackson is sitting there thinking about the number of times he's seen me and how many of them involved a sign of this damn sickness. I'm feeling mighty embarrassed. But I'm hoping Jackson ain't the type to clear out when things get rough.

"Time is it?" I ask, trying to sit up, and well, change the subject.

"Eleven," Mama says. "How you feeling?"

"Better." Ain't nobody ever stayed over in the hospital with me and Mama before, not even Dog.

She looks back and forth between us and says, "I'ma go get a cup of coffee. Y'all want anything?"

"I'm starved. We didn't get much of a chance to eat at the picnic," I say.

"I'll see what I can scrounge up." And then, she actually leaves us alone.

I smile at Jackson, wondering if I look like death warmed over. "So much for playing it cool."

He laughs and hangs his head.

"She giving you a hard time?"

"Just watching out for her baby girl. Nut'n wrong with that. You okay?"

"Yeah. That was real nice of you to stay. Mama must think we been seeing each other a long time."

"I kinda sorta told her 'bout the times we seen each other. I hope you don't mind. I didn't exactly have a choice. Once you went out, she was ready to send me packing if I didn't tell all."

"Figures," I say, wondering how much exactly he said, not that there's anything to hide. It's just there's some stuff you want to keep private. "Think she'll lock me up the rest of the summer?"

He smiles. "I reckon so. I'll just have to break you out every now and again so's you don't wither away."

"Guess I ruined the picnic, huh?" I imagine all them folks talking about us after we left and likely making a fuss about me and Jackson.

"Ruined it? I believe you saved it from being a total washout. Didn't you say you wanted to give 'em sump'n to talk about?" he teases.

"Very funny," I say. "What must they think?"

"Who cares," he says, all somber.

"You don't?" I ask.

"Not a lick," he says.

"And you don't care about my age?"

He looks as serious as a heart attack and he says, "Listen here, girl, alls I know is I came out here this summer feeling like my life was done finished. My daddy up and died without warning. My mama's a mess. She's carting me out here like she don't wanna have to deal with looking at the spittin' image of her dead husband all day. And I got to contend with my rich, snobby kin treatin' me like crap. And then one day I see this cute girl with sump'n special goin' on behind her eyes. In a matter a days, she goes and saves my life, in more ways'n one, and you want to know do I care that she's two and a half years younger'n me? Would it matter if you was twenty and I was twenty-three?"

It's a damn good thing they're pumping those steroids into my veins or you can be sure I'd be in the depths of another attack. It's just what I meant when I said he was real. I don't believe I ever heard anybody talk like that before. And holy hell, Mama is standing in the doorway hearing it all, too, a tray full of food in her hands.

I can see Jackson's embarrassed, wishing he'd kept his mouth shut. And all I want to do is take that away for him.

"I'm glad you're here," I say. "I'm sorry it took your daddy dying to bring you out this way, but I'm so happy you came." Mama steps back out and closes the door. I lean towards him and we kiss, and it's just as sweet as it was under the tree at the picnic. And Lordy I forgot where we're at! The heart monitor starts to beeping, and Mama and the nurses come rushing in lickety-split. We're caught red-handed. Jackson starts to blushing, and I'm turning near about purple. But then Mama busts out laughing, and I think I ain't never seen a better day, happy as a clam at high tide.

7

Rules for Savannah and Jackson's Courting
[Mama actually wrote this!]

1. Y'all are not to be alone in the house together under any
    circumstances. This goes for the Channings' house, too.

2. When at either house, the bedroom door is to remain
    open at all times.

3. The back of the Channing boys' truck is off-limits—
    period!

4. Y'all are not to be out at the beach after dark.

5. Savannah's curfew is 10 o'clock during the week and 11
    o'clock on weekends. *[Like it would even matter whether
    it's the week or the weekend during summer vacation!]*

6. Savannah may spend time with Jackson only after her chores are done. *[I knew that one was coming.]*

7. Finally, y'all best mind your manners. I've got eyes watching for me just about everywhere. Don't cross me.

Now if that ain't the most humiliating manifesto you've ever seen, I don't know what is. Can you imagine? Mama sat us down before we even left the hospital to go over this little document with her. I honest-to-God thought I might die of embarrassment! Jackson blushed something fierce but didn't say a word against it. It must be awful. Here he is eighteen years old and more or less free to do as he pleases, and now he's saddled with a list of rules as long as his arm. I'm surprised he didn't up and hightail it out of there.

Just as Mama was finishing up her little tirade, the bald-headed doctor came in to tell me about the new medicine I'm supposed to start taking every day. I kept trying to tell him that the asthma doesn't come every day. But he wouldn't listen. He said since I ain't managing it with my inhaler, I've got to try this. As if it's my fault. As if it ain't the damn asthma that's managing me.

I'll say one thing, that attack sure done brung everything out in the open. Now Mama, the preacher, all them church folk, and God himself know all about me and Jackson. Somehow, it turned us into an official couple. We just skipped right on past the rest of the getting-together phase of things. Not like with this one guy I had a crush on last year. It took about a century for him to notice me and another decade for us to get together. Then it was only a matter of days before he went and broke my heart, just moved on to the next girl. I reckon Mama's aiming to protect me with all those rules. I sure was a mess after I got dumped. But damn, does she know how to complicate things.

For example, I don't know if you ever tried it, but a hammock ain't no place for a romantic encounter. Here me and Jackson are just a couple of days after I got out of the hospital, laying in the hammock, with the lightning bugs flashing their tails at us, the moon shining bright, stars starting to peek out from their hiding places. Sounds near about perfect, don't it? I'm laying with my head on Jackson's chest, just listening to the sure, steady beat of his heart. He tips my face up to his and we kiss and, damn, it's sweet. But when he tries to turn towards me and the hammock starts to swinging and his feet get caught in the rope, it's all I can do to keep us from tipping.

According to rule number one, we can't be in the house alone together, and Mama's still at work. But the mosquitoes are biting and so are the chiggers. The humidity is so high I feel like somebody done left the hot shower on all night long. Still, there ain't nothing better on this earth than kissing Jackson Channing. And just as he starts running his hand over my shirt, I hear Mama's car drive up. On the one hand it sucks real bad, 'cause now we can't be alone, but on the other, at least we can go inside and escape the bugs and the heat.

"Vannah, you here?" she calls.

"Yes, ma'am," I reply, as we come out of the shadows towards the house.

"Y'all want to come in and watch a movie?" she asks.

My mouth is watering for more of what we've been doing, but what choice have we got?

"I reckon," I tell her as we head inside.

"Dog get off to Dave's okay?" she asks.

"Gina came and got him," I answer.

"Y'all have a nice evening?" she asks, eyeballing Jackson.

"Yes, ma'am," he replies in a croaky voice, squirming.

When she heads off to the bathroom, I put a movie in and cuddle up beside Jackson on the couch, hoping she might go spend some time in her room. But she's back, making herself comfortable right beside us.

"What movie did y'all choose?" she asks, like we're having a little get-together with her.

"*Star Wars*," I say, trying to hold my grin. I know she hates those movies, and Jackson, like all guys, will probably love them. Personally, I could take them or leave them. But I know Mama won't have too much patience for this one.

Out of the corner of my vision, I can see her looking at Jackson.

"How's your mama doing?" she asks.

Durn, that woman ain't got no sense! He doesn't want to be talking about his grieving mama!

"Fine, I reckon," Jackson replies.

"And your brothers?" she asks.

Jackson shifts uncomfortably.

"Mama," I say, "did you not invite us in here to watch a movie?"

"All right! Just trying to make conversation."

I glare at her and she smiles, picks up *People* magazine, and starts flipping through it. "You watch the stories today?" she asks me.

"Like I have time? You know I got a list of chores could keep a body busy till dark if I let 'em. You think I'ma waste my time on a bunch of soap operas?"

She shakes her head. "I never get a chance to watch my stories, just wondering what all was happening."

I put my finger to my lips, silently telling her to shut up so Jackson can watch in peace. I love my mama, but damn, can she be a nuisance when she wants to be. She goes back to flipping through her magazine.

Inch by inch, Jackson moves his hand, so it's on my back against my skin.

"Y'all want something to eat?" Mama asks, jumping up.

I sigh, wishing she'd just go on to bed. I'm about to yell no, when Jackson looks at me all desperate. "I could eat," he says. Boys are always hungry.

Mama steps into the kitchen and starts banging things around.

"You want me to fix you a sandwich?" I offer. Then I change my mind and whisper, "Let's go into town and get a burger and a shake." 'Cause suddenly I feel an intense need to get out from under Mama's thumb.

"How we gonn' get there?" he asks. He's got his driver's license, but no car. I ain't got neither.

"We can ride bikes," I suggest. "You can borrow Dog's."

"What about the movie?" he asks.

I just look at him.

"Okay." He smiles. "Let's go."

I call to Mama. "We're gonn' go get some burgers and stuff out at Eddie's." That's the main diner in town.

Mama looks at the clock. "You only got about an hour till curfew," she warns, looking hurt that we're leaving. I shrug. "Don't be late!" she hollers as we head out.

We sit across the table from each other, staring into each other's eyes. This is way better than some old space movie. We've got two straws in our strawberry shake, just like in a picture.

"What's wrong?" I ask Jackson, noting the down-turned corners of his mouth.

"Nut'n." He half smiles.

"Come on, don't lie," I say, hoping he hasn't grown tired of me already.

"My ma's been calling."

"What about?" I ask.

"I reckon things are hard for her. Carter and Tyler keep getting into trouble, and my dad ain't there to set 'em straight." He sighs. "First she don't want me around 'cause I remind her too much of him. Now she wants my help in his place."

Lois brings us our food. Her hair, which is very big, is forever changing colors. Today it's ruby red. "Here y'all are," she says. "Enjoy."

"I like the color," I say, pointing at her hair.

"Why thank you, sugar," she replies, patting it gently. "Sweet of you to notice."

I pour a pile of ketchup on my plate and salt it up real good. Then I dip my fries in one at a time.

Jackson chuckles. "Most people put the salt on the fries."

"Well I ain't most people," I say.

"That's for sure true," he replies, but I can tell by his smile he means it kindly. He eats some of his burger, then looks at the Elvis clock ticking on the wall. "Things was easier before."

"Before your dad passed, you mean?" I ask.

"Yeah, that. But also before . . . you know, all them rules and whatnot."

"You mean before Mama's manifesto? I know. I told you we shouldn't let her know about us."

He shrugs, looking forlorn.

"Tomorrow's Saturday. I get a break from chores," I say. "We could spend the day at the beach."

"That sounds right about perfect," he replies.

"What your cousins gonn' be up to?" I ask, wondering if he wouldn't ruther be off running around with them.

"Usual dumbass crap," he replies.

Nope, I reckon he wouldn't, I think with a smile, glad they haven't pulled him into their bullying richy-rich gang.

He lights up. "Hey, come surfing with me tomorra."

"I don't know how," I say, though the idea seems exciting.

"I'll take you on my board," he says. "I'll teach you." Mama'd have a fit if she knew. But my asthma's been good since I started the new medicine.

"I'd love to," I say.

"Meet me soon as you get up," he says. "We'll get an early start. Meantime, we best get you home. You got fifteen minutes." He leaves some money on the table, then holds the door open for me on the way out. As we ride, he looks over through the dark every couple of minutes just to smile at me.

We crunch into the gravel driveway at exactly eleven o'clock on the nose and set the bikes back in the carport. Jackson leans up against me and kisses me real deep. My insides turn to jelly. But then the outside light flips on.

"Curfew," Mama calls, sounding none too happy.

I hug Jackson tight and wave good night. Then I walk on in right past Mama without even saying a word. My mind is already floating on that surfboard somewhere out in the sea.

I get up at first light Saturday and tiptoe around, careful not to wake Mama. I want to be good and gone by the time she rises. I'd ruther wait on Jackson down there than risk her holding me up. I make sandwiches and put them in my backpack along with some green grapes, potato chips, and cold lemonade. After taking my medicine, I pack my inhaler and slip on outside in my hot pink two-piece swimsuit. The pavement is already steaming, which doesn't bode well for the heat this afternoon. But leastways we'll be out on the water. I'm so excited, I forget the sunscreen and towels. I creep back inside, careful not to slam the screen, and get that stuff quick as I can.

I see him down by the water waxing his board. Damn, he looks fine, his chest muscles bulging and the sun glinting in his wet hair. I lock up my bike and run down to him.

"'Bout time you got here," he chides.

"It ain't but seven thirty!" I reply. "When did you come?"

"Crack o' dawn." He stares at me like I'm his dinner, and you remember what I said about boys being hungry. It's like in them cartoons when the cat is looking at the bird and suddenly it appears to be a roast chicken. "Couldn't sleep."

There are only two other people on the beach. And though I'm tempted to lay down with Jackson in the sand, you know one of them folks has just got to know my mama.

"How 'bout that surfing lesson," I remind him.

"Cold water'll do me good." He laughs. "Wait here and I'll show you a time or two." He paddles out to where the waves break. He catches a good one. But then he's showing off, trying to look cool, and next thing you know, he's falling facefirst into the water. Lucky for him, the board goes the other way ruther than hitting him on his head. I cover my mouth, but I can't help but giggle. He comes out of the ocean all dripping and blushing.

"Some teacher you gonn' be." I laugh.

"I just got a bit ahead o' myself is all. Come on, I'll take you out." He reaches for my hand, but I ain't so sure I'm wanting to try it after all. I don't want to be falling and looking foolish like that.

"That's okay," I tell him. "I believe I'd ruther sit and watch awhile."

"Come on. Don't be chicken," he teases. But I back away, smiling, and run down the beach. He runs after me, tackling me to the sand. And then we're kissing and law, everything seems perfect.

"Savannah, that you down there?" I hear a voice calling. I look up and good God a'mighty, it's Mr. Howard, my third-grade teacher, wearing Bermuda shorts with black socks, a tank top, and a fishing hat. I sit up right quick.

"Hey, Mr. Howard."

"Well, I'll be, Savannah Brown. You sure have grown. Why I just saw your mama, wadn't but last week. She told me you were coming up, but I didn't realize you'd grown so."

You know he's going to run straight to Mama aiming to get into her good graces. I always did think he had a crush on her, and now here's his excuse to call her up.

We get on up out of the sand. "It has been a long time," I say, looking for my way out. "If you'll excuse me, sir, I was just about to have a surfing lesson, so we'll have to catch up later on. Take care now." I grab Jackson's hand and tear on down the beach, the both of us laughing ourselves silly. Jackson takes his board and we splash out into the ocean.

Past the wave break, where the water is deep and calm, we hang on to opposite sides of his surfboard. It's quiet out here, and Lord have mercy, we are actually alone.

"Sorry about that," I say, "us being interrupted and all."

"Don't worry. It's kinda funny, ain't it?"

I just love that about him, how he can see the humor in a situation. I hop up across the board and kiss him on his salty mouth.

"Savannah Brown," he whispers.

"Jackson Channing," I whisper back.

A seagull screeches overhead.

Jackson looks up. "He know your mama, too?"

After a while, he rides me to shore on his board—him standing towards the back, me on the front on my knees. It's way more exciting than Boogie Boarding. So I decide to give it a try.

He drops the surfboard in the sand and shows me how to jump up onto my feet on it. I'm just glad there ain't too many people out yet. I expect I look awful silly.

"I reckon you're ready to give it a go," he says, clearly having more faith in my abilities than I do myself.

I paddle out and he wades in beside me. He anchors the board until a nice, gentle wave comes, then launches me into it. I hang on tight as I can.

As the wave crests, I let out a little shriek without meaning to.

"Now!" he yells.

So I jump to my feet, which sends the board out from under me, and I belly flop into the shallow water. I come up sputtering, and he laughs.

"You okay?" he asks, grabbing the board and my hand.

I nod, not too sure I want to try again.

"Come on, now," Jackson says. "You just got to land with your feet evened up is all."

So I give it another go. This time I nail the landing and manage to stay on my feet for a good five seconds before I wipe out. "Did you see that?" I call when I come up.

"You did it! Woo-hoo!" he yells.

I take a couple more turns, then collapse on the sand.

"What's wrong?" he asks.

"That's hard work!" I reply. I'm beat, but it's been real fun having Jackson for a teacher. "You go on. I want to watch you."

So he goes out and catches those waves like a pro. He seems to know how to read them, become a part of their motion, whereas I'm just standing on the top of them hoping they're not going to buck me off.

By the end of the day, I'm able to actually stay up all the way to shore. I never imagined I'd be able to learn so quickly. Course I'm only catching the baby waves, but still.

When we're fixing to leave, he says, "You want to go watch the fireworks with me on the Fourth?"

"Sure," I say, "long as Mama's okay with it and all."

"My cousins are having a party afterwards at the house. My aunt June and uncle John are gonn' be out of town for the night."

"I'll check with Mama. I reckon I won't mention the out-of-town part."

"That sounds like a good idea."

Imagine a Wonder Bread like me at an upper-crust, upperclassmen party. Stef and Joie would flip!

8

I wait until the morning of the Fourth before finally broaching the topic of my plans with Jackson. I've taken the risk of asking Mama while she's getting ready to head to the Family Dollar, so if I can get the yes, she won't have a chance of taking it back since she's working late. But so far, it ain't quite going my way.

"It's a weeknight," she says. "Curfew is ten o'clock."

"The fireworks won't even start until nine thirty! Only babies are gonn' have a ten o'clock curfew tonight."

"You are a baby—my baby—and I ain't too keen on the idea of you going to this party. Them boys are too old for you." Imagine what she'd have thought if I'd mentioned the parents weren't going to be there.

Just my luck, Dog stumbles in from our bedroom in his boxer shorts, his hair all bedraggled. "Did I hear you say we got to be in by ten on the Fourth of July?" Dog demands. "Gina's letting Dave stay out until eleven thirty! Fourth of July is the best night of the year! If you say ten, I'ma just go stay at Dave's."

Mama struggles to get her too-tight work shoes on, looking more irritated by the second. "Eleven thirty is too late for a twelve-year-old," she says. But I can see the pressure is getting to her. "Where are you planning to be out so late?" she asks him.

"Me and Dave were invited to a party," he says.

"Where at?"

"A friend's house."

"What friend?"

"Just some kid we met down at the beach."

"Do I know his parents?"

"Forget it. I'm sleeping over at Dave's."

Mama sighs, beaten down, and finally caves. "Eleven o'clock for the both of y'all. And there had better not be any drinking going on at these parties, y'all hear me?"

"Yes, ma'am," I say, and run out of the room before she can change her mind. Guess I owe Dog one.

Jackson and I meet at Eddie's for dinner, then walk down to the beach to wait for it to get dark. It's crowded as hell down there, everybody trying to get a good spot to watch the fireworks. Junior and Billy Jo have got blankets spread out in the back of their truck, which is parked right in the middle of the sand. They're trying to lure a bunch of girls up with chips and beer.

"You want to set up there?" Jackson asks me.

But I just keep hearing Mama's rules in my head. And even

though there's all these people around, I know I ain't supposed to be in the back of that truck under any circumstances. Plus them boys get mean quicker than a drunk in a bar fight, and I reckon the beer's going to help that right along.

Jackson looks at the goings-on in the truck and says, "I believe I'd ruther walk some if that's okay."

Lord am I relieved! We walk and walk, but there just ain't no privacy to be had on the beach tonight. After a while, though, the crowds thin out and we've got a little more room to ourselves. He sits down in the sand and I plop down between his legs, my back to his chest. A shock of excitement hits me as my body touches his. But the humid air makes it too warm and sticky to fully enjoy a cuddle.

I'm thinking about how Mama let me come out here, knowing full well we'd be down at the beach after dark. Granted the whole town is, too. But maybe I might could consider this to be implied consent that rule number four is no longer in effect.

Jackson seems awful quiet.

"What you thinking about?" I ask.

"Nut'n rully," he says. "Mama called again today."

"How come?" I ask.

"Tyler got caught shooting out a streetlight with a BB gun. And Carter's been skipping summer school."

"They keep on getting into messes, huh?"

He nods.

"What does she want you to do about it?"

"I don't know. She can't seem to decide which is worse, having me around or not," he says, sounding heavy. But then he leans down and kisses my neck real gentle. Right at that very moment the fireworks start with a big old *kaboom* and I feel just like that—exploding with light.

The grand finale is my favorite—all those colors bursting into the sky amidst all that ruckus, then the sudden stillness. Afterwards, we wait awhile for the crowds to clear out, then walk up towards the Channings' place holding hands. I wore my nicest miniskirt and a fitted tank and tried to do my makeup to make me look older. Truth be told, I ain't feeling too comfortable about this here party. I walk extra slow. We won't be able to stay too long anyhow, 'cause of my curfew.

We can hear the music from the party a mile away. When we get there, it's blaring so loud my ears are ringing. Junior and Billy Jo high-five Jackson and look me over like stray cats on a can of sardines. The house is seriously swanky—plush carpet cushioning the floor, polished wood banister curling up the staircase, family photos in gold frames glinting on the walls, glass and chrome bookshelves holding fancy bric-a-brac, and a baby grand piano gussying up the living room. The air conditioning is blasting full on. Some of the girls are turning up their noses at me. They're all dressed up like this here's the Red Carpet or something. I didn't realize it was going to be so fancy. The guys are all wearing shorts and polos. And Billy Jo has on his Mudcats cap.

"This is Savannah!" Jackson shouts over the music to no one in particular.

"We know Puddles!" Billy Jo hoots. And there it is—ancient history coming back to bite me on the butt. Ain't nobody called me that in ten years. I reckon he's just trying to make the point that I don't belong here. At our school, you've got the rich kids, the poorer kids, and the farm kids. There just ain't no mixing between groups. I don't know what I was thinking coming here, knowing I'd be the only one who didn't belong.

Junior smacks Billy Jo upside the head. "Lay off it," he demands, and pushes a beer into each of our hands.

There are serious amounts of liquor being consumed. A bunch of guys have brought 40s, and most of the girls are drinking wine coolers. But some of the kids have busted out everything in the parents' whisky cabinet. Drinking games are being played already, too. We walk through the house towards the backyard. In the kitchen, kids are smoking cigarettes and weed. The room's so full of smoke, I start coughing and wheezing.

Jackson takes me out back. They've got a swimming pool! There are kids swimming in their clothes and a few stripping down to their drawers. Couples are starting to go at it in every nook and cranny of the yard and patio. I'm feeling like a dumb little kid and a big old dork both and just trying to focus on calming down my lungs. Once they get irritated, they like to stay that way.

Come to find out Billy Jo has followed us out here. He has definitely had too much to drink. I reckon he started his party down at the beach.

"Want another beer, Puddles?" he taunts, though the one Junior shoved into my hand is as of yet untouched. "Afraid you can't hold your liquor?" Snorting and laughing, he pitches himself onto the ground.

"Piss off, Billy," Jackson growls through gritted teeth, and leads me away from his obnoxious cousin. "Come on. I want to show you something."

We go inside and down the steps to the basement.

"Woo!" some kids call out as we head down, as if they're assuming we're about to do you-know-what.

Most of the basement is a finished rec room, with a big-screen TV and a foosball table and darts. But Jackson leads me to a section off in the back that's unfinished—like a wood cave with a sink and a concrete floor. Inside, he goes over and pulls a sheet off of three of his paintings that are leaning up against the wall. They take my breath away.

"Jackson," I whisper, my hand over my mouth. "These are amazing." Like something you'd buy in a store. There's one of the sun setting over the ocean, and it feels all eerie and sad somehow. And I know it must have come from his own imaginings, seeing as the sun only sets over the sea out west. The next one, I'm guessing, is his dad catching a football, a big smile on his face, and he just seems like the father every one of us would want, like you can feel the love and acceptance shining in his face. The last painting ain't quite finished yet, but I can tell it's going to be of me! I can't believe how he made my eyes light up, and even my hair looks good. "You are seriously talented." And even though I knew in my heart he would be, I can't help but feel shocked by the extent of it.

He shrugs. "I'm a'ight."

I shake my head and kiss him.

But then a bunch of kids come down the stairs, laughing and tripping on the way.

"Come on," he whispers, as he covers the paintings with the sheet. "I'll show you my room."

But when we get up there and open the door to the guest room, come to find out, there's not one but two couples in there.

"This room's full up," one of the guys calls out in an angry voice.

"Let's go," I say, wanting to just get out of there.

Without a word, Jackson leads me downstairs and towards the front door.

"Y'all aren't leaving already, are you?" Billy Jo calls. "We were hoping to see a puddle!"

I'm trying real hard to turn the other cheek and yank Jackson towards the door. But he spins around and points his finger at Billy Jo. "I'm warning you."

"Let's get out of here," I whisper to Jackson. We don't take but one step towards the door before Billy Jo starts chanting, "Pud-dle! Pud-dle!" And then a whole mess of them kids are joining in. All them seniors I'm going to see at school in the fall, and every one of them either remembering or finding out about me peeing my pants when I wasn't but five years old! It ain't like I was the only one it ever happened to, it's just it was out in front of everybody on the way to the school bus. I'd been holding it all day, afraid to go use the school bathroom by myself. And finally, I just couldn't hold it one solitary second longer. And here I am ten years later and it's still haunting me.

Jackson turns my hand loose. He strides over there and he punches that Billy Jo right in the nose. "Don't you never speak to her again, not as long as you live."

Holy hell! We need to clear out and quick. Billy Jo's on the floor, and everybody's swarming around him, and Jackson just breezes over, takes my hand, and walks me right out the door and on down the road. And suddenly the humid night air doesn't feel too sticky or nothing. I'm just grateful to be out in it.

"Sorry 'bout that," Jackson says, looking downright miserable and rubbing his hand.

"S'okay," I reply, overwhelmed by the whole thing. I ain't sure whether to feel honored that he defended me or shocked that he went and hit his own cousin or sickened by the sight of blood or scared of what might could happen next.

"There's gonn' be hell to pay tomorra when my aunt and uncle get home," Jackson says.

I hope Junior will stick up for him and let his parents know that Billy Jo provoked that punch. I hate to even think about all the damage them kids are causing to the house. Least Jackson ain't responsible for that mess.

We pass by Town Park Playground and I look longingly in at it, though I haven't been inside in years. Maybe I'm just missing a simpler time of life. I reckon Jackson must have caught my brain wave, 'cause he pulls me in there and nudges me up on the red twirly thing me and Dog used to call the merry-go-round. I stand in the middle and Jackson pushes me around faster and faster. I close my eyes and hang on, feeling dizzy. I open them back up when I hear him jump on. He wobbles, then makes his way over to me in the center.

"What you think they'll do?" I ask him, wondering how strict his aunt and uncle are.

He shrugs. "Let's don't think about it tonight."

"But you hit him," I say, then shudder, even though it ain't cold out.

"Ain't nothin' real but this," he whispers back. Then he leans in and kisses me as the world spins past us.

I come home to find Mama bundled up under the cotton throw on the couch, sniffling, her eyes all red and puffy.

"What's wrong?" I ask.

"Nothin'. You know me, just crying over spilled milk." The shoe box of old photos of her and my daddy from way back when is on her lap. She's holding a picture of the two of them on his motorcycle, her arms around his middle, her face resting on his shoulder, and another one of him lighting a bonfire at the beach, his eyes all lit up.

I plop down beside her and pat her hand. I reckon she was lonely tonight. "How come you didn't go out with Gina?" I ask.

"She had a date," Mama says, wiping her nose with a Kleenex.

"Seems like a long while since you had one of them," I say, hoping that doesn't hurt her feelings.

"I'm too tired," she says, though I ain't clear if she means to date or to talk about it. "Go on to bed. I'm waiting up for Dog. You have a nice evening?"

I ain't at all sure how to answer that. "I reckon," I say, and slip off to my room before she has a chance to ask what I mean.

"Jesus, Mary, and Joseph! Dog, I'm gonn' give you a lickin' if you don't quit working my last nerve!" I can hear Mama hollering up in the house.

I'm out here lazing in the hammock, 'cause my breathing was raggedy all night long from the smoke at the party. I'm so dang tired this morning. Good thing I don't have to be at work until the afternoon.

Mama doesn't seem to mind me being idle as long as Jackson ain't around. But give me one second with him here and suddenly the carport needs hosing down and the cellar's got to be swept out and who knows what all else! Thank the Lord it ain't autumn yet or I'd be raking leaves morning, noon, and night.

Lucky for me it was Dog who was late coming in for curfew last night, so he's the one in the doghouse, so to speak.

The phone is ringing, and I just know it's Jackson, 'cause all the little blond hairs on my arms are standing up like I've been hit by lightning. I've got to try and get to it before Mama. I'm positively dying to find out what happened once his aunt and uncle got home today.

No such luck. Mama's already chatting him up when I come through the door. I reach my hand out, but she's blabbering away about food like a durn fool.

"Mama, he don't care what you fixed yourself for supper last night! Give me the phone. Please," I add, hoping to curtail her jawing. Damn, I wish she'd just go on and get me a cell phone. Maybe I can use my work money on that.

"Savannah's near about ready to yank my arm clean off if I don't hand over the telephone. Y'all keep it short now. I'm expecting a call from Gina."

I rescue Jackson from Mama and sneak off to the laundry room to talk to him. He's just invited me to the beach, saying he's got to tell me all about what's happened with his aunt and uncle in person, when Mama's call comes in. I can't even tell by Jackson's voice if he's got good news or bad.

"Hang on," I tell him. "I got a beep." Sure enough, it's Gina. And I realize I might could use this to our advantage. I switch back to tell Jackson I'm on my way, then chat Gina up but good while I change into my swimsuit. I hand Mama the phone on my way out the door. "I'ma head to the beach," I call, as the screen slams behind me.

"Vannah!" she yells. And I can hear that she's pissed I'm slipping out 'fore she has a chance to give me any jobs to do. "Don't be late for work and stay on our side of the beach and . . ."

I wave as I ride my bike down the street, trying to get out of earshot before she comes up with some dang chore I need to get done, like spinning yarn into gold or some such nonsense.

9

I can tell right away things didn't go well. Jackson's sitting on the sand looking forlorn.

"What happened?" I ask.

He shakes his head like he can't even speak. Finally he explains. "There was all this damage to the house—a busted chair and spills and a cracked tabletop. Billy Jo told 'em *I* threw the party. *And* I broke his nose. So my aunt and uncle say I've got to go. Plus my mama called and said she needs my help with the boys anyhow. She's coming to get me tomorra mornin'."

I'm so stunned I can't hardly breathe. "How dumb do they got to be to not notice who's got a hangover and who doesn't? This can't be right!"

He wipes the tears that have suddenly sprung from my eyes, takes my hand, and sniffles himself.

"We got to fight this," I insist. "Won't Junior stand up for you? You've got to explain."

But he just shakes his head. "I need to go pack. I'll call you later on." He gives me a quick kiss and then he's gone.

I ride over to the library and clock in, then go to the bathroom and sob. This just can't happen.

Miss Patsy knocks on the door. "Savannah? That you in there? We've got books waiting."

I'd like to tell her off, but instead I go out and slam those books onto the shelves. She steers clear of me, not being real big on emotional outbursts herself.

When I get home, I see a note from Dog saying he's staying over at Dave's. Mama's working till closing and then has a staff meeting. There's a message on the machine from Jackson saying he'll call me later when he can. I sit by the phone, writing out all my anger in my journal and waiting. By the time the telephone finally rings, the sun has already set.

"Can you meet me at the beach?" Jackson asks.

I don't give a rat's ass whether or not the rules are still in effect, dark or not dark, I'm heading straight down there to see him one last time. I run out and jump on my bike. Can't hardly see the road from all these dang tears coursing down my face.

There he is. My heart does a funny little leap in my chest. I drop my bike and run straight for him. We kiss, and he feels all warm and strong.

I shake my head, trying to find the words. "You just can't go," I tell him. And his eyes are all glassy in the moonlight like he's wanting to cry, too. "Ain't there any way we can change their minds?" I beg.

He shakes his head. "Already tried."

"But you're eighteen," I remind him. "Can't you just refuse to leave? Maybe you could stay with us."

He sighs and turns to look out to sea, just like he used to when we first met, which, in truth, was only a matter of weeks, even though it feels like I've known him my whole life. "You know your mama wouldn't stand for that. Plus, it ain't just about them kicking me out. My ma regrets sending me off. She needs my help. You know how it is," he says, "my daddy up and dying and all. She can't handle Carter and Tyler on her own. And I can earn a living working some job or another."

"But your painting!" I cry, knowing he was meant for better than working in some factory or convenience store.

He just shrugs. "It'll have to wait, I reckon."

We sit down on the cool sand in the dark and hold hands, not saying a word.

"My asthma's been so much better," I whisper, wondering if Jackson's being here has somehow broken the spell of my daddy being gone.

"It's that new medicine you been taking every day. Fixed you right up."

"I reckon," I reply, though I ain't at all convinced. "Can't you get a job here and send the money back home?" I ask, knowing his answer before he even thinks it himself.

He shakes his head. "You know I done wore out my welcome with my kin, and like it or not, ain't no way your mama's gonn' let me stay with you. I got nowhere else to go."

"You didn't do nothing!" I argue.

"Not accordin' to Junior and Billy Jo."

I can't stand thinking of him taking the blame when those boys threw that wild bash and Billy Jo brought that broken nose on his own dang self.

"What if I can't breathe without you?" I whisper ever so quiet. Everything inside me seems to be closing in on itself. I can already picture all those little bronchiolies in my lungs getting small.

He hears the shift in my breathing as I start to cry and turns to face me. "Use your inhaler," he says.

I breathe in the mist, but I know it ain't what I need.

He takes my hands and looks into my eyes. I see the moonlight reflected in his.

"I don't want to go," he croaks out. "I hate the idea of leaving you." He looks right frantic. "Don't go thinking I'm like your daddy, taking off and unreliable. I ain't like that, y'hear?"

"I know," I say, stroking his soft hair. And we both of us know there ain't a damn thing we can do to change the situation. So we just lay back on the sand, listen to the surf, and stare up at the stars. I got my head on his chest and our legs are all intertwined and I wish this moment wouldn't never end. And one of my feelings comes over me—one of those itty bitty moments when time seems to freeze—just for a breath. And I get the feeling that this moment fits, matches somehow, with something from the future. And I know this ain't the last I'm going to see of Jackson Channing.

"It's gonn' be okay," I tell him. "This ain't the end."

"You sure?" he asks, sounding like a scared little kid.

"Yeah," I tell him. "You ain't rid of me yet."

And he leans in and gives me a kiss that reaches right down inside of me and stirs something I never even knew was there. I'm about ready to jump his bones when I see the headlights in the parking lot. And I ain't got a speck of uncertainty about whose car it is.

"That'll be Mama," I say, getting choked up.

"I love you, girl," he says, all breathless.

"Good Lord, Jackson," I say, fanning myself. "I love you, too."

And then Mama's there dragging me off, squawking about how I done broke rule number four and how she ain't never going to let me out of her sight again. And blah, blah, blah. But my eyes are fixed onto the outline of Jackson's body and I can sense the pull of his eyes on mine. And truly, don't nothing else matter.

10

"Vannah, I will not have you mopin' about the rest of the summer. Boys come and boys go. You may as well learn it now. I know you're all tore up about him leaving, and seeing as you're brokenhearted and all, I'ma cut you some slack. But I'm telling you now, I ain't gonn' have you setting there like a bump on a pickle the rest of the summer. So go on and lick your wounds and then get over it."

She's one to talk—still pining over my daddy, and he's been gone near about twelve years. But this ain't the same deal at all. Jackson didn't run off on me. He loves me. He done told me so. It's just his mama needing him at home and his stupid kin tossing him out like the trash.

Maybe I might could move out there. Go to high school in Green-ville. I could help his ma with the cooking and tending to the boys— even if they are about my own age.

"You need something to keep you busy. You got a reading list for school?" Mama needles me.

"No, ma'am. It's summer *va-ca-tion*, as in no homework," I say, even though I've been reading *Jane Eyre* between trashy romances in my spare time.

"Perhaps Miss Patsy can make some suggestions so you can get ahead for the fall."

Always pushing. She knows I don't need to be getting ahead. Don't I deserve a break? I go flop down on the couch.

"What about your workbook?" she calls.

Somehow, since I met up with Jackson, I seem to have let it slide. And now, I can't even bring myself to care. I sure wish Stef and Joie would get home.

Gina stops by, and she and Mama sit in the kitchen drinking coffee.

"How's she doing?" Gina asks, like I'm not sitting ten feet away.

"She's setting there looking like the last pea at pea-time." Mama laughs.

I want to explode, feeling like don't nobody in the world under-stand my pain. Ain't nothing I can do about it neither. I done explained the whole thing to Mama about the party and all. She ain't sure what to think, though she ain't too happy about Jackson being the one who threw the punch.

The phone rings and Mama picks it up. "Hello?"

"Is it him?" Gina asks. "Let me talk to him."

Mama giggles and pulls the phone away. "Come on, now," she says, pushing Gina aside. "It's for you, shug."

I look up from where I've been studying the design in the old shag carpet in the living room. I never noticed before how the swirls had a pattern to them.

She brings the phone over to me. I hold my breath, afraid to hope. Then she nods with a smile.

I jump up and grab it. "Jackson?" I say as I step outside into the yard.

"Hey, baby," he says. And I tell you, them words melt me right into the ground.

"Dag, I miss you something fierce. I can't believe it's only been two days."

He sighs. "Me, too."

"What's it like being back there?" I ask.

"It's a'ight," he says.

"Your mama mad about you punching out your kin?" I ask.

"Naw," he replies. "Boys'll be boys."

"That's good," I say, breathing a sigh of relief.

Then there's just all this dead silence on the line.

"Say something," I beg.

"What?" he answers.

And my heart sinks right into the red clay dirt beneath my feet. We ain't never going to make this work if we can't talk to each other on the phone.

"Don't be like that," I beg.

"Look, I got to run. I just wanted to hear your voice is all."

"You got a job yet?" I ask just to keep him on the line a minute longer, but end up sounding like a naggy housewife.

He hesitates. "Mama wants me to put in an application at the auto body shop. Thinks the money'll be good." He sounds like somebody done up and stole his puppy.

"What about maybe painting houses?" I suggest, all gentlelike. He doesn't answer. "There must be house painters in Greenville!" I can hear him smiling. "You just take that telephone and call every painting company out there and tell 'em what they'll be missing out on if they don't hire you. Jiminy Crickets, boy. Don't make me come out there and explain it all to your mama myself."

"You are one crazy-ass girl, Savannah as in Georgia."

"I miss you something terrible, Jackson as in Mississippi."

"I'll call you soon," he says.

"Love you," I say, sounding too hopeful.

"Back at you, baby." And then he's gone and I feel even worse than I did before.

11

I can't breathe. I just woke up from a dream where my daddy was sitting on my chest watching me struggle for air. But even though I'm awake, I still can't get a good breath. I'm shivering even though it's hot.

My asthma's been acting up the last few days. Mama says it's the pollen. She'd like to keep me indoors all day long if I'd let her. She ain't even close to right. Even though I know in my heart that Jackson wouldn't have left me if he'd had his druthers, my asthma doesn't know that. Alls it knows is that somebody done up and went.

I've been coughing myself awake on and off all night. But now I feel it coming on for true. I hate to wake Mama, but I expect I best hurry before I can't get up at all. I'm leaning forward, trying to gulp down some air.

"Dog." Why am I whispering when I'm trying to wake him up? "Dog!" I yell-cough.

"Ungh," he grunts.

Now I'm sweating, feeling panicky. "Dog," I wheeze again, and I am fighting for air.

He picks his head up off the pillow. "D'you use your inhaler?"

"Yeah," I croak, grateful he's awake and comprehending the situation.

"Mama!" Dog yells, sitting full up in the bed and staring at me like my head might just pop off. "Mama! Vannah can't breathe!" And to my surprise, he sounds right concerned.

Mama comes bolting in, her jammie top falling off the edge of her shoulder. Her hair's all a wreck, and her face doesn't look too good neither. She tears over to the bed and starts shaking me real hard, then yells at Dog to move his ass and call 911. Only thing I can't figure is why I feel like I'm hovering up on the ceiling looking down at myself, unless, holy s-h-i-t! Am I dead?

I'm too young to die. I ain't even had a chance to find out what all everybody is so durn excited about when it comes to, well, you know, the birds and the bees and all that mess. I didn't even get to say good-bye to Jackson. Now that ain't hardly fair.

Oh man, Mama is freaking out. "It's okay. I'm all right," I try to tell her. But even though I can hear the words in my head up here, they don't come out of the mouth she's looking at down below.

"Has she been taking her medicine?" she barks at Dog.

"How should I know?" he yells back.

"Did she use her inhaler?" she cries.

"Yes!" he yells, triumphant. "I asked her right before I called you in. She said she did."

"Y'all calm down!" I try to say. But when I look at myself, I can see I'm not saying a word. "Lord, it's gonn' be all right." Except then I notice how my lips are looking blue.

"Where is that G.D. ambulance?" Mama shouts. "I'ma give them one more minute, then I'm toting her off to the hospital myself."

Meanwhile, my poor body is passed out and struggling for air. Mama's holding me all tenderlike and telling me to hold on. Aw, Mama, don't cry.

She's on the phone telling Gina to meet us at the hospital. She's got one arm around my body with her hand on my chest, like she's feeling my heartbeat. Dog looks like he's fixing to be sick himself.

I've got to say, it is nice to know they care.

It's strange being out here instead of, you know, in there. I'm just watching it all happen without being concerned about any of it, except for the fact that I ain't in my body. That part is sincerely creeping me out.

"I hear the sirens!" Mama shouts.

I feel myself drifting higher than the ceiling. Up there I'm walking on a bright path, and right in front of me is a hand-painted sign on an old slab of wood hanging from a post. There's sand blowing around it. The yellow letters spell out two words: HOUSEPAINTERS NEEDED.

I start to drift away from it. The ambulance dudes down below rush in and put a mask on my face and start pumping air into me. I try to stay focused on that sign, wondering what it might could mean. But then I feel a jolt of some kind, and everything goes black.

∽ ∽ ∽

There's something strange down in my throat making me feel like I'm drowning. It's choking me. I drag open my eyes and turn my head to see Mama asleep in the recliner beside me. I can't seem to breathe when I want to. And then air gets pushed into my lungs when I didn't mean for it to. It's a terrible feeling, not being in control of my own body, and I am in a serious panic. Somebody moves on my other side. I twist around to see and law! It's Jackson! Now I know I must be dreaming. That boy is all the way up in Greenville.

I try to call out to him, but I can't make nary a word come out of my mouth. They've got some kind of tube running down my throat, and it's making it hard to breathe or swallow. I ain't never had to have that before. And there's a bunch of machines beeping and moving. This must have been a bad one. I can't even remember what happened.

"She's awake," Mama says, pressing the nurse's call button. "Don't try to talk, baby." She looks spooked, like I just rose from the dead or something.

I make my eyes bug out to tell her I ain't at all happy about this.

"I know," she says. "Hang on just a sec."

The door opens, and I'm expecting old baldy from my last hospital stay to march in. But it's a young doctor, and as I look at her name badge, I discover I ain't even at Mercy. It's got the Wilmington logo on it!

Dr. Arletta Jones has smooth, dark skin and a bright, sunny smile. "How you feeling?" she asks me.

As if I could tell her if I wanted to. Does she not notice the big, fat hose they done stuck into me? *If you'd take this here pipe out my throat, I might could tell you I feel like I been chewed up and spit out,* is what I'm thinking. But I ain't exactly got any way of communicating it.

Jackson takes my hand in his and Lordy, part of me just melts. But I'm in too much of a panic to really enjoy it.

"All right, hon, if you can relax, we'll remove that tube. Otherwise we'll have to sedate you," Dr. Jones says.

I squeeze Jackson's hand real hard, 'cause I'm scareder than a worm on a hook when the fish are biting. He holds my hand in both of his and brings it close to his mouth.

They sure know how to kill a moment. Next thing I know, they're yanking tape off my face and pulling this big old nasty tube from my throat, and it feels creepy coming up out of me like that. And it makes me gag. Luckily there ain't nothing in my stomach to come up along with it. That there is just about the worst feeling I done ever felt. It leaves me wore out and, somehow, ashamed.

Then something comes to me, like remembering a dream, foggy at first, then coming clear—the image of a sign—yellow paint on a wood slab, saying: HOUSEPAINTERS NEEDED.

I cross my fingers, hoping it means what I think it might. I smile up at Jackson, relieved now that they got that awful tube out, and tears pour right from my eyes. I don't even mind them sticking the little bitty oxygen prongs in my nose. "You're here," I try to say to Jackson, but don't one single sound come out, not even a croak.

"You done scared the bejesus out o' me, girl," Jackson says.

"I'm sorry," I say without making a sound, but secretly I'm tickled that I actually found a way to get Mama to bring Jackson to me. I turn to her. "What all happened?" I try to ask. Nothing but gurgles and chokes come out, though I manage to mouth the words. I grab at my throat.

"Your voice should return in a couple of hours," Dr. Jones explains. "The tube pushed your vocal cords apart. They'll be back to normal soon enough."

"I'll tell you what happened," Mama cries. "You near about died, that's what." She's shaking her head and catching her breath like she's about to bawl herself.

"Let me listen to your lungs, Savannah," Dr. Jones says, pulling out her stethoscope, which is cold as a witch's tit. After listening for what feels like forever, she turns to Mama. "Don't worry, now. She'll be okay. We need to keep her here a couple of days to work out the meds and see if we can figure out what set her off, so we can all feel reassured this won't happen again. In the meantime, let's give her plenty of rest and keep the emotional ups and downs to a minimum, since we know that's one of her triggers." She glares at Jackson.

I'm fixing to get all pissed off, thinking she's suggesting Mama send Jackson on home. Then I realize my angle. Only I still can't talk. I tap Mama's arm and gesture for her to hand me an ink pen and some paper. I write: *Jackson best stay close by then, 'cause if he leaves I'm going to be a mess.*

"Clever," the doctor replies, smiling. "I'll have to watch out for you. Ms. Brown, if I could talk to you out in the hall for a moment."

Usually that burns me up when they leave me out of the discussion, since it's clearly about me. But today, all I can think is I got a couple minutes with Jackson all to myself.

I wait till they close the door. *How'd you get here?* I write on the paper.

"Your mama called." He sounds serious. "I believe she thought you was gonn' die. Probably figured me being here might give you something to hang on for."

See there? She knows it as well as I do. I need him. The image of that sign pops into my head again, and come to think of it, wasn't I up on the ceiling when I saw it?

"You was pretty bad off."

How long you been here?

"Since yesterday. Your mama called me 'bout five a.m., shortly after they brung you in. I tore out the house with barely a word and drove here fast as I could in my daddy's old truck."

I set down the pen, hold his hand and bring it to my cheek.

He leans his face in close to mine. "Don't do that again," he whispers. "I couldn't take losing you."

The chills run all up and down my spine, my arms, and everywhere. I don't want to nag, but I suddenly can't help myself. I grab the pen and paper again and start scribbling what's on my mind. *You've got to come back, Jackson. Greenville is just too dang far off. I can't hardly stand it. You've got to come paint houses. There's this sign with yellow paint somewhere and I believe they're waiting for you, and . . .* My breathing's getting raggedy and my nose is stinging from wanting to cry. This writing business is too slow, and I can't get across how desperately I need him to come on back.

"Hush, now. You have another fit and your mama will surely send me packing. Breathe, girl."

I lay back, holding tight to his hand, and try to set my breathing to rights. Mama and the doctor come in. Dr. Jones puts the nebulizer on me so the mist and medicine seep into my lungs. She glares at Jackson, but he doesn't look at her. Pretty soon I'm breathing good again, but I'm plumb wore out. He waits till the doctor steps away, then starts stroking my hair.

Once the doctor leaves, Mama squints up her eyes and looks from me to Jackson. "I appreciate you being here with her," she says to Jackson. "You're a good boy."

How embarrassing. He's eighteen years old!

"I've been thinking an awful lot about what Savannah said happened at that raucous party," she continues. "I got to tell y'all, I'm wanting to believe her that you didn't have a thing to do with it. Am I right?"

"Yes, ma'am," Jackson says without hesitating.

Mama nods. "What about that fight?" she asks.

"I'm sorry, ma'am," he says, standing up tall, "but I ain't gonn' tolerate nobody pickin' at Savannah. We tried to walk away three times, but my cousin just wouldn't quit. We were aiming to leave when he just pushed it one step too far."

The nurse comes in right then and makes me breathe into one of them plastic peak-flow doohickeys that measures how hard I can blow air. I'm wishing she would go on and leave, 'cause I'm dying to hear Mama's reaction to what Jackson just said. I'm huffing and puffing into that clear tube, making myself right dizzy, though the little red marker inside isn't hardly rising. Finally, the nurse takes it from me and checks my vitals. *Get!* I want to yell at her.

Soon as she steps out, Mama picks up the conversation right where we left off. "You want me to try to talk to the Channings for you?" she asks in a low voice.

Now ain't that sweet?

"That's a'ight," he says. "Best we just give 'em some time to cool down, I expect."

"That's real mature of you," Mama says. Then she nods at us and looks towards the door. "I'ma go enjoy the afternoon sun. Y'all behave."

I pull on the back of her shirt to get her attention, then write, *Maybe you should go to work. Jackson's here to look after me.*

"You let me worry about that," she replies, her smile tight.

I shake my head hard, knowing she's going to lose her job again. Then she turns and walks right out of the room.

But now me and Jackson are on our own. Granted it ain't exactly like a whole lot can happen. But it's time to ourselves nonetheless.

Somehow I just got to make him see how important that yellow sign must be—to the both of us. He's just got to go looking for it.

When Mama comes back, I raise the issue about her job once more. *It's really okay. You can go on to work,* I write on my notepad. I can tell by her wrinkled-up forehead she's worried. Plus she's got dark bags under her eyes, and she keeps on biting her lip.

"I appreciate your concern, Van. But Jackson does not know your usual meds and dosages, and he is not qualified to make your medical decisions. We'll do all right. I called Miss Patsy and told her you were under the weather. So your job's safe. Now quit your worrying."

Why don't you tell your boss the same thing? I write.

"Wouldn't matter if I did. I haven't got any sick leave."

She tries to smile, but I know she's worrying, not just over the job, but also on how we'll afford our end of the costs. All I can do is try to get well right quick. I lay back, close my eyes, and breathe.

12

*J*ackson's mama wants him to hurry on back home. He ain't even been here but three days. Poor thing's been sleeping in a recliner chair by my bed every night. First she sends him away. Then she calls him back. Now she can't even get by for just a few days without him? He's got this clunky old cell phone she gave him, and it's ringing every few hours.

She says he needs to get on home and see to getting himself a job right quick. He doesn't want to leave. He's still all worried about me, 'cause Dr. Arletta Jones says I'm going to have to stay in the hospital for a few more days, and he figures that can't be good.

Somehow I've got to get him to go look for that wooden sign with the yellow paint. He ain't left my side once since he got here, which is sweet as hell, but I need him to find that sign!

He says he ain't got time to drive along the coast to look for some imaginary sign. But I believe it's the way for us to stay together. He wants to kowtow to his mama and go work at some old machine shop or some such nonsense instead of painting, which he and I both know is what he is meant to do. At least painting houses is closer to his true calling than a body shop. Plus, when he was out by us, he had time to paint pictures, too.

Dr. Arletta Jones keeps on picking at me to make a list of what kicks off my asthma. It's simple, really. There's dust and pollen and mold and fertilizer. There's feeling mad and stressed and overexcited. But here's what it comes down to: My daddy left and my breathing quit on me. Jackson came into my life and it eased up. He left and I quit breathing again. The solution sure seems clear to me. Jackson's just going to have to move back out our way.

Only problem is, don't nobody believe me. When I tried to explain it to Dr. Jones, Mama laughed out loud, saying she just said that when I was little 'cause she was pissed at my daddy. Maybe, but that don't mean it ain't true. She doesn't believe I remember him leaving, but I do, and just thinking about it gets my chest all choked up.

I wake up early, the light coming in through the blinds dim enough to be dawn. Jackson's face is just inches from my own. He's standing over me.

"You 'wake?" he asks.

"What's wrong?" I answer, sitting up quietly so as not to disturb Mama.

"I got to go. My ma called again. Tyler done run off. She needs me."

"*I* need you," I say, knowing I'm pouting, but unable to help myself.

"Come on, now. It won't be forever."

"You're supposed to find that sign. I just know you are," I tell him.

"I ain't got time to be chasing some dream sign." He can see I'm hurt by that one. "You know I trust your special feelings. They done saved my life."

I don't tell him that ain't technically true. I saved him from the train 'cause I was out there spying, but it sounds good, so I let it lie.

"I ain't got a choice here. I got to go." And I can tell he's all tore up about it, so I let him off the hook. But I can't help my tears spilling out. "Be strong, Savannah. For me?" Then he presses his lips to mine. I grab on to hug him and don't want to let go.

Mama stirs. "What's going on?" she asks, all confused.

"I'm leaving, ma'am. Mama needs me back home."

She looks over to me, sees I'm a wreck, and sighs. "All right, baby, come on," she says.

I hug him real hard and let go as tears flush out of my eyes as if pumped from a well. I bite my lip so's I don't make no sound.

Jackson hangs his head and walks to the door real slow.

"At least give me your cell phone number so I can call you on it," I say.

"It was my dad's. I gotta give it back to my ma soon as I get home."

He gives me a sad smile, then he's gone and I just bawl my head off. All that crying gets my lungs worked up. That's one of the things I hate about this here asthma. Every time I get to feeling something, just wanting to be left alone with my pain, all them dag bronchiolies in my lungs decide to get tight and then Mama makes a federal case of it, calling in the nurses and the doctor, and I can't even have just a minute to myself to grieve.

13

*B*ack home, I crawl out of bed at ten one morning to stop the dang phone from ringing. "Hello," I say, all irritated.

"It's me, grouchy!" Stef laughs.

"Dag, I missed you. Seems like you been gone a lifetime. July is nearly half over!" I say, rubbing the sleep out of my eyes.

"Seriously," Stef agrees. "I got so much to tell you."

"Me, too," I say. "You won't believe it. I met this guy named Jackson. He's sweet as can be. He's kin to the Channings, eighteen years old. And things were going so good between us and then . . ."

"I've been with someone, too," she interrupts. "At camp. His name's Jimmy. He's our age, and girl, I think I may be in love. It was killing me that phone calls weren't allowed there. I was dying to tell you about him."

"I know what you mean. But things have gotten all messed up with Jackson now. His mama made him move back out to Greenville!"

"How do you think I feel? Jimmy lives all the way down in Georgia! At least y'all are in the same state."

Somehow this is not making me feel any better. I try again. "He's a painter, Stef. He showed me some of his paintings, and they're just amazing. He was planning on earning a living out here painting houses till he can do something with his real art. But his mama got him to take a job fixing cars. Ain't that just a shame? She don't think house painting would make him good money. And that ain't even true, least I don't think it is."

"That sure is awful," Stef says, finally seeming to understand my predicament. "Come meet me at the swimming pool and we can catch up."

"I'm working at the library in an hour. Meet me over there. We'll hide from Miss Patsy in the stacks and talk."

"See you then."

While I'm shelving books, Stef charges me with a hug, her blond ponytail wagging behind her. She's wearing cut-off jean shorts and an oversized camp T-shirt with a picture of a lake and some trees, signed all over in Sharpie by her friends. I sure am happy to lay eyes on her. We sneak deeper into the rows of books where we can talk.

"You're peeling," I notice. Stef loves to lay out, but she's got that fair skin that is forever burning.

"Me and Jimmy liked to go canoeing on the lake."

Suddenly the green-eyed monster has me by the throat, imagining her and her boyfriend just drifting idly on the water with no grown-up worries about money and jobs and parents needing help.

"He's the real deal, Vannah. I don't believe I've ever felt like this about any guy before." That *is* saying something. Stef has had loads of boyfriends. "We went swimming together and laid out during free time. He taught me to do archery, can you believe it? I'm not half bad either. And we went to the dance together on the last night."

"You're so lucky," I say.

"He's such a sweetheart, too. There was this one time, we were on a hike, and there was this big muddy patch and he threw down his sweatshirt for me to step on, just like in the movies!"

Suddenly, we hear the jangle of bangles and hold our breath. Miss Patsy waddles up to our row and clears her throat noisily, staring us down. Strangely, I find that I'm not at all saddened by the interruption.

"I better get back to shelving books if I'm ever going to get out of here."

"You didn't get a chance to tell me about Jonathan," Stef says.

"It's Jackson!"

"Sor-ry," she says.

"I reckon it'll have to wait. Some of us have to work." I smile so she doesn't get offended.

"I work! I'm babysitting for the Parker twins this afternoon. Then I'll be twenty dollars closer to my goal for the car I'm gonna buy when I turn sixteen. But if you want to come with me, I'll go halfsies with you on the babysitting money like usual."

"That's okay," I say, not a lick interested in spending all afternoon with a couple of hyperactive seven-year-olds.

"Joie gets back from Florida tomorrow. Maybe we can all go to the fair the next day," she says.

"I don't think I'll be able to go," I reply.

"Why not?" she blurts.

I shrug. I just ain't in the mood this year.

Stef sighs, gives me a hug, and traipses off. "Call me!"

I hate to say it, but that girl was riding on my nerves.

Mama and I are spending our evening in front of the TV. I'm hoping Jackson will call. She's drowning her depression in a quart of rocky road. She always gets like this when she loses her job. I damn near begged her to explain about my asthma. But she wasn't hearing it. She sure can be stubborn. Now I can't tell whether it's the unemployment she's upset about or back to my daddy leaving or everything together.

She's sitting over there on the couch in a hideous flowery housecoat, fluffy pink slippers on her feet like it's the dead of winter, flipping through her magazine, sighing.

She talks about how my daddy left her high and dry and tries to act all chummy with me, like we're in the same boat. But I tell you, this boat here is a yacht compared to her dinghy. We ain't the same at all. Jackson loves me, and he *is* coming back. Sometimes I wish Dog was home more in the evenings instead of being out with his friends. At least when he's here we just focus on the TV without all the chitchat.

"Stef's mom called today. Said Stef and Joie are planning to go to the county fair tomorra," Mama says. And I know she must know that I declined their invitation, so I don't say nothing. "Sure sounds like fun."

I try to act like I'm focusing real hard on the TV, though I haven't a clue what this show is about. It's one of them summer pilots of a new series, but I haven't paid a lick of attention all night.

"All them rides, corn dogs, cotton candy . . . Savannah!" She sits up. "I'm talking to you."

"I ain't interested in the fair," I say to settle her down, but I keep my eyes on the screen.

"Since when?" she shoots back at me.

It's true. Generally speaking, I'm a pure T sucker for the fair. But this year I just don't feel like it. I shrug. "Prob'ly won't be good for my asthma. All them critters and whatnot."

"That one's gonn' come back to bite you on your butt," she warns. "You best hope Jackson don't invite you out to a farm or a rodeo, 'cause you sure ain't going."

We sit quiet for a minute, her staring at me, me staring at the TV.

"Come on, Vannah," she says. "It'll do you good."

"Why don't you go?" I snap. "Maybe it'll do *you* good!"

"Now that's enough," she says.

"How long *you* been sitting on this couch?"

I can see I done crossed a line by the pulsing of the vein in her temple. She's going to blow. We square off. I try to look tough and contrite at the same time, which is near about impossible. I reckon I hit a raw nerve.

"Don't you disrespect me," she says, looking like I might have chosen the wrong moment to do so. "Maybe you'd like to be on punishment, Miss Sassy. I suggest you go to your room and you can forget about going to the fair or anywhere else *or* talking to Jackson for the next two days. How's that?"

Her voice sounds sort of shrill. If there's one thing I know, it's when to cut bait. I head to my room, not caring about any of it, except not talking to Jackson. But lately our phone conversations seem awful dry anyhow. Maybe it'll be good for us to miss each other for a little while.

I take out my journal and doodle images of Jackson. It's his eyes I fix on, the eyes that draw me in. Can't hardly find the way to show that special look in them, that look I first saw out at the beach when he smiled at me.

Dog comes busting into the room, just back from his evening out. "Mama's taking me and Dave to the fair. Too bad for you. I hear you're on punishment."

Jackass. I stick my tongue out at him. Very mature, I know, but it seems to suit the moment.

"Mama!" he cries like a two-year-old, "Vannah stuck her tongue out at me." Then he smiles, all evil.

"Good Lord!" Mama calls.

I put on my headphones, crank up my music, and pull out my current romance, *Bedazzled by the Butler*. For now, that's the only escape I got.

14

alking down the beach, I watch the waves roll in and
back out, just like they did the day me and Jackson
had our surfing lesson. But today, the waves seem too loud, the warm
sand under my feet too hot.

Mama, Dog, and Dave ran into Stef and Joie at the fair yesterday. I
reckon I'm an idiot for turning them down in the first place. All this
sadness over missing Jackson just makes me grumpy. Don't nothing
seem to catch my interest lately. Mama was so sick of me hanging
around the house all gloomy, she said I can go do whatever I please.
But I'm still restricted from phone calls until tomorrow. I'm strolling
down the beach, searching for some peace.

Usually when I walk out here all by my lonesome, I prefer to
head down where the sand turns white and the beach is lined with
all them fancy vacation homes. But today I'm going the other direction, where the sand looks like dirt and the beach property like a

shantytown. Don't ask me why—suits my mood, I reckon.

There's a whole mess of broken glass strewn about. I've got to watch my every step. Mama might just shit a brick if she's got to take me back out to the hospital.

Right after they got back from the fair yesterday, she got herself a new job cashiering over at the Harris Teeter Grocery, just a twenty-minute ride down the coast. Put on her high-necked flowery blouse and a long skirt, looking the part of the good Southern mama, and made her case, promising to be reliable and all that when she knows perfectly well ain't nothing changed. Still, it ain't like there's all that many folks lined up by the "help wanted" signs. I reckon it's either her or some high-school kid. Seems to me like the fair did her good after all.

It's quiet out this way without all the tourists—no big ol' ladies in their too-small bikinis, their brand-new straw hats blowing off their heads, no young'uns with a whole big laundry basket full of sand toys and beach balls, not to mention rafts and kites, Boogie Boards and floaties.

I see Stef and Joie by the water before they see me. The two of them were friends for years before we were all in the same class in fourth grade. Sometimes when I see them together, I still get a twinge of feeling left out, wondering why they didn't call me. I guess I shouldn't be surprised, since I wouldn't even go to the fair with them.

"What are y'all doing out this way?" I say.

They run up and give me hugs. "I was just telling Joie how I was afraid you were gonn' mope around all summer," Stef says.

"How was Florida?" I ask Joie. She looks tan and relaxed, her brown curls lightened by the sun.

"Real fun," she smiles, giving a broad view of her buck teeth. "Sorry I couldn't call you. My mom wouldn't let us make any phone calls from my cousins' house."

"I thought y'all were getting a cell phone."

"We did. But my mom insisted on getting the plan with the least number of minutes and then wouldn't let us use the dang thing! What is the point of that, I ask you?" She sets her hands on her boney hips.

Stef is the only one of us who has a cell phone. It's ridiculous. Especially with my asthma, I should at least have one for emergencies.

"I'm having people over to watch a movie at my house this afternoon. Think you can come?" Stef asks.

"I'm supposed to work," I say, which is a sincere lie, but I just ain't in the mood for a bunch of immature kids today. Still, I don't want to hurt nobody's feelings.

Stef may be on to me, 'cause she says, "I thought you get to choose your own hours."

"I do, but once I choose them, I've got to stick by them."

"You want to go get a Coke with us?" Joie asks sort of timidly, like she's expecting me to say no.

"That's okay. I believe I'm just gonn' walk awhile. I'll see y'all later on."

And I keep going down the beach. I reckon I was rude, and to my two very best friends, too. But I'm just wanting to be by my lonesome today. I haven't talked to Jackson for days and it is sure making me miserable.

Jellyfish season seems to be upon us. I done passed three in a row—the big, fat kind that look something like a brain sitting there on the sand. They give me the willies. I never understand how kids can go up and poke at them with a stick. Makes me want to toss my cookies.

The birds are calling something fierce; sounds like they're having an important meeting if you ask me, everybody yelling and getting on each other's cases.

All this walking is sure making me tired. Least I got the cool ocean breeze to keep me going. I've near about had it. But I've got this nagging feeling inside, you know how sometimes you just want to finish something. I can see the end of the beach from here. And it doesn't look too far, although looks can be deceiving. It's probably another mile or so at least. But I've come this far, and I just can't give up now. I'd go home feeling worse than when I started.

I've lived out here my entire life and never walked all this way. I can do it, just keep my eyes focused on them big jutting-up rocks at the end.

The sound of construction comes on pitiful loud, giving me a big ol' headache. I'd heard there was hurricane damage out here last summer. But I didn't realize they were rebuilding already. I feel sorry for the folks still living here, what with all that noise. I sure would like to turn back and get away from it. But them rocks are so close now—spitting distance is all.

Sure wish I'd brought something to drink. I'm panting like a dog.

As I reach the rocks, ruther than plopping down in the sand as I'd imagined I would, I decide to climb up to the top, celebrate my victory. And dang is it worth it. Sitting up here, I can look out over the sea like a bird. It'd sure be peaceful if it weren't for that God-awful racket them construction folk are making.

I look back there to see what all they're building, and Lord have mercy, there's my sign—yellow letters, wooden post, just like I saw it up on the ceiling!

I trample down the rocks and run up to the trailer to inquire.

"Howdy," I say to some dude with a caterpillar mustache who's sitting behind the desk. "Y'all looking for painters?"

"You a bit young to be looking for work, ain't you?" he says, smoothing down his comb-over. The scent of Aqua Velva is over-powering—just like at school dances.

"It isn't for me," I assure him. "It's for a friend of mine. He's the best painter around. He paints beautiful pictures. He's just doing houses till he gets famous." I've got to calm down or he'll think I'm carrying on like a crazy person. "Have you got an application I can take him?"

He eyes me a minute too long, like he ain't sure he buys it. But then he searches through a mess of papers on his desk and hands over the form. "I need somebody to start next week. Job should last a good few months. Might be sump'n else down the line if'n things work out."

"Yes, sir," I say, nearly busting out of my boots from excitement. "Next week would work just fine. Thank you kindly." And I race my butt down to the beach and jump around like I really am out of my mind. I start running towards home, can't wait to call Jackson and tell him the good news. My punishment may not end till tomorrow, but Mama will have to cut me a break for something this big. Law, Jackson ain't going to believe it! Imaginary sign indeed.

I stop to breathe. I've got five or six miles ahead of me. I'm going to have to take it slow. But then I look behind me toward that yellow sign and I know it was worth it, every dang step.

15

*B*y the time I get home, dusk is near upon us. To my relief, nobody's at the house. Mama would have a fit for sure if she knew how far I walked. Now the question is do I call Jackson and hope Mama doesn't find out, or do I wait and try to get consent? I reckon it's easier to ask for forgiveness than permission.

I take the phone to my room and dial Jackson's number, which I've got good and memorized by now. Only his mama answers and says he's still at work. Durn!

"Please tell him Savannah called and that it's very important. I'd appreciate it if he'd call me back ASAP."

"All right, then. But y'all are running up my phone bill. He's gonn' have to pay for that, y'hear?"

"Yes, ma'am," I reply. "And how are you doing today?" I ask, remembering my manners and hoping to make a good impression.

"I'm just fine," she says, without any effort to further the conversation.

"And how about Tyler and Carter?" I ask.

"They're all right. Nice talking to you, but I've got to run now," she says.

"Remember to tell Jackson I called, please," I add as she rushes off.

I set the phone down and just stare at it, waiting for it to ring. Did you ever notice that when you do that, it's a pretty sure guarantee it ain't going to happen? I try sending my brain waves at it, willing it to ring for what seems like forever. Then, when it suddenly does, I about fall off the bed.

"Hello!" I pant, my heart racing.

"Savannah Georgina Brown!" comes Mama's voice. "You ain't supposed to be picking up this phone when you know good and well you're still on punishment, unless you hear my voice come on the machine."

Shoot! "Sorry," I stammer, trying to come up with something quick. "Stef said she might have some kids over and you said I could go where I wanted and I thought it might be her." That seems convincing.

She hesitates, I expect while she turns that one over in her mind. "All right, I suppose you can go, I'm just calling to say I'ma be late. Can you fix supper for the both of y'all?"

"Dog ain't here," I say. "Ain't seen him all day."

"Where's he at?" she barks.

"I expect he's with Dave, where he's always at. How should I know?" I bark back.

"All right," she sighs. "I'll be home 'fore long. You have a good day?"

"It was okay," I say, just as I hear a beep on the phone. "Is that all?" I snap, anxious to click over.

"I was trying . . . ah, hell. I'll see you later then," she grumbles, and clicks off.

I mash down the flash button. "Hello, hello!" I yell, praying he hasn't hung up.

"Savannah?"

Shew! It's him! "Jackson! You got to come down here! I found the sign! The wooden one with the yella letters, just like I said. It's all the way out by Morehead. Can you believe I walked all that way? Anyhow, I got you an application. And the man said they need people to start next week. So I'm sure he'll hire you. You just got to come fill out the application and then you can move back down here." Okay, I know I rambled on there, but I am positively floating on pride. The sign is real. And I found it for him! I'm near about ready to bust!

But there's just pure dead silence on the other end.

"Jackson, you there?" I say, thinking maybe we got cut off.

"I'm here," he says, real quiet.

"Well, damn, boy, what's wrong? Didn't you hear what I said? I found the sign. This here's what you're meant to be doing."

"Vannah"—and I can tell by his voice this ain't going to be good—"I cain't just up and leave."

"Why not?" I say, as my big balloon of excitement deflates into a little old useless piece of rubber. "You got things straightened out with your brothers, and you'd be making money to help out. . . ."

"Mama still needs me here. And I'm expected down at the body shop."

"But don't you see? That sign has got to be important, don't it? Jackson?"

Somebody's beeping through on the other line, but I ain't answering it. Time seems to have stopped, as I wait for him to speak.

"Sorry," he says real soft. "Look, I got to go. I'll call you tomorra."

"Wait," I say, trying to keep him on the line till I figure out how to convince him. "You done any painting since you been home?"

He's real quiet. "I hadn't had time."

"You had time here. Don't you want to get back to it?"

"Look, I really got to go. We'll talk soon." And he hangs up, just like that.

I cut off the light and climb under the covers in my clothes.

You know how them mobsters like to tie a person to a big ol' concrete block and drop them into the water? That's just how my heart feels—sunk.

Mama barges in and flicks on the light. "Good Lord, Savannah! What are you doing?"

I look up at her with my tear-blotched face.

"What in the world happened?" she asks.

I just shrug.

"You were fine when I spoke to you not half an hour ago."

I'd like to answer so she'll leave me alone. But I've got all these desperate feelings inside of me, and I can't figure how to explain it all. It's like when my breathing won't let me get air in. Only now my feelings won't let me get them out, like they're all stuck inside my chest.

"Talk to me," she demands. "Did something happen with Stef? Are you ill? Do I need to call the doctors?"

I shake my head from its perch on the pillow.

"Jackson?" she asks, dang mother's intuition.

I nod.

"When you were supposed to not be on the phone?"

I nod again and start in to bawling.

"Well," she sighs, "looks like you already been punished for that one by the looks of you. Come on, now. It ain't the first time your heart's been broken."

Oh, like that helps.

"It wouldn't hurt so durn bad if you weren't such a hopeless romantic. You set your expectations too high, shug." She sighs and pats my back. "You had any supper yet?"

I shake my head.

"The better looking they are, the less you can trust 'em," she mutters, then heads off to the kitchen to do her motherly duty of feeding me, while I hide under the covers, wishing I'd never been born.

16

The next afternoon I'm sitting on my bed, trying to figure out what else I can possibly do to fix this. I couldn't stay in the living room with Mama another minute. She's driving me up a wall, gaping at me like she's trying to show she knows how I feel. This here is totally different than her broken heart.

After all the trouble I've been to, after I went and found that sign, proved it was real. How can he not jump into his daddy's truck and speed on down here? I understand his mama is having a hard time and all and I don't mean to be unsympathetic, but seems to me she should be able to handle two nearly grown boys on her own. She needs to let Jackson get on with living his own life.

I know he misses me. Maybe he'll come around. But by then, it'll be too late for the painting gig. So it's up to me to fill out this here application for him, get him that job, and convince him he can still help his family from here. Then he can come on down to the coast and get back to his two true passions—painting, and me, of course.

Whew! Am I glad I figured that one out. Now I know just what I've got to do.

Name: Jackson Channing. I best try and make the handwriting messy, so it'll look like an actual guy did it. I'll put down his kin's address and my phone number. If they called his house and his mama answered, she might have a conniption. I know his birth date, but I'm going to have to get creative with the work history. It won't be too tough. I know he currently works at the body shop, that he used to help out his daddy making cabinets, and that he paints pictures. No, he ain't never been arrested! Good Lord, they ask some strange questions. Available start date? I expect he'll come around by next week. Yep, that should do just fine. I address the envelope to the P.O. Box listed on the application and go out to the kitchen to get a stamp.

I'm feeling better already. Mama always says action soothes the sore soul. I reckon she's right.

"Sure is nice to see you looking so chipper." Mama's been acting overly nice since my little sobfest last night. It's worse than when she's mad at me. She's treating me like I'm in kindergarten. But now that I've got Jackson all sorted out, it doesn't even matter.

I go stick the application in the mailbox and come back to sit at the table where Mama's drinking coffee and puzzling over bills on her day off.

"How come you haven't been spending time with Gina lately?" I ask.

She looks at me like she hadn't realized I'd come back in. "What now?"

"You mad at Gina or something? How come y'all never go out anymore?"

She peers into my eyes like she's aiming to figure out if I'm trying to get rid of her or something. Then she shrugs. "I'm tired, Savannah. I ain't got energy for all that silliness no more. Face it, girl, your mama's old."

"Thirty-six is old," I agree, "but it ain't like retirement old. Why don't you get out there and meet some folks?"

Suddenly, she looks irritated. "Why don't you try finding a new job every few months, working all day, coming home to do the wash and the cooking and cleaning and settling fights between you and your brother, not to mention fretting over all these bills, and then see do you feel like going dancing." And with that, she storms into her bedroom and slams the door.

Shoot. I was only trying to help.

Tuesday morning, I'm laying in the bed with hours to go until I need to be at the library. I can hear Mama getting ready for work. Dog's snoring, as always, when the phone starts in to ringing.

"No, there's no Jackson Channing here. How did you get this number?" Mama's saying.

Holy hell! I leap out of bed and tear out of the room. "It's for me! Give me the phone," I insist.

But Mama shakes her head. "I just can't understand why he'd give y'all this number. It don't make . . . oh, I believe I'm getting it now. Could you hold on just one second?" She gives me a look that says I had better have a damn good explanation.

"Please," I beg, reaching out my hand for the phone.

She holds my gaze another minute, then relents with a sigh, handing over the telephone.

"I'm sorry about that, sir. It was just a misunderstanding," I explain. "I can take a message for Jackson."

"This some kinda prank? Y'all pulling my leg or sump'n?" the man asks, sounding irritated.

"No, sir. I've got a pen ready. What was the message?"

He hesitates. I could spin him a yarn, as the old folks at church would say, to try and explain, but I think I'd best keep quiet at this point.

"If'n he can show up down here at my trailer tomorra, he has himself a job."

It worked! He actually got it! "I'm afraid tomorrow isn't a possibility," I say, stalling for time. I bite my lip to keep myself from screaming my excitement out loud. "He's got another painting gig is all. How about Friday?" Surely he can get down here by then.

"A'ight, then. We'll see him on Fri-dee."

Hot dog!

I set the phone down and look up to see Mama glaring at me, her arms crossed against her chest. She raises her eyebrows as if to say, "Spill it."

"What?" I ask, trying to sound innocent. She keeps her stance. "I just got him a job is all, painting houses, like he wanted. Is that so awful?"

"And, why, may I ask, ain't he down here doing that for himself?" she asks, tapping her toes.

I shrug. "'Cause his mama's always holding him up. I don't understand why she can't get on without him. She's the one that sent him off in the first place."

Mama looks shocked and disappointed. "I am surprised at you! Not having a lick of respect for people who have lost someone dear to them! I'd of expected more, young lady. I suggest you forget about this boondoggle of yours and get back to the business of living your own life." Then she shakes her head and goes off to her room.

It ain't that I don't feel bad for Jackson's mama. I just don't think she should use it as cause to ruin her son's plans. He's got to move on and find his own way, not try to replace his daddy.

Am I being selfish? Of course I am, who among us ain't? That doesn't change the fact that my aim is to set Jackson on his own path, the one he was meant for. After all, a vision that comes to you when you're half dead has got to mean something important, don't it?

I keep calling his house, but ain't nobody answering. Something must be wrong with their machine. Where could they be at? Finally I go to work, but I can't seem to concentrate. Miss Patsy quickly gets fed up with my air-headedness and starts following me around to make sure I shelve the books correctly. This snaps me out of my zoned-out behavior, as I cannot stand for her to be looking over my shoulder like that. When I finish, I head straight back home. Jackson must be in by now.

No such luck. I intersperse my phone calls with working on my SAT book to keep myself distracted. The longer I call, the more worried I get. I hope he's all right. As the day darkens to night, I lay up in the bed, listening to music, dialing and redialing his number. I go and make sandwiches for me and Dog for supper, leaving his next to him while he watches the TV. I eat mine in our room.

Mama's tired when she gets back from working at the Teeter. I get a tub of hot water for her feet, which I try to do whenever she's looking particularly weary. It helps take the edge off her mood. She soaks them awhile, then slips off to her bedroom. Dog and I watch TV. Then he goes to bed, too. I keep redialing. Finally, near about midnight, Jackson answers. I'm so glad to hear his voice after all them hours of redialing, I don't even pay attention to the dark tone in it.

I mute the TV and blurt out, "Hey, Jackson! It's me."

He sighs. "What you doing calling so late?"

"I been trying to get you all day. Where y'all been at?" I don't care if it's nosy. At this point, I believe I've got a right to know.

"We went up to Greensboro to visit my grandma. She been real sick."

"I'm sorry." I never know what to say when people talk about someone being sick or dying. I mean what can you say? Sorry? It ain't like I made her sick. Changing the subject sometimes helps. "Why'd y'all come home so late?"

"Mama didn't want to leave, but me and her have to work in the morning, and Carter's got summer school. Why you calling at this hour, anyhow?" He sounds impatient.

He's probably tired is all. Maybe I should hold up and talk to him about all this tomorrow.

"I'll let you go. I just wanted to be sure you were all right."

"That why you called at midnight?" He doesn't sound convinced.

"There was something else, too. But it'll keep. I'll call you tomorrow."

"You got me now, may as well go on and say it."

I know I ought to hush my mouth and stay my tongue. But I can't seem to help myself. I spill the beans. "'Member I told you about that sign? About how I found it and all?"

"Savannah, I told you I cain't do nothing about that right now."

"I know," I say. I'm in too deep to back out now. "That's why I took care of it for you. I got you that job painting houses, Jackson, just like you wanted. Alls you got to do is be down here by Friday. That'll give you a couple of days to explain it all to your mama and drive back out here. And then it'll be perfect." He doesn't say a word. "Ain't that something?"

After an awful long silence, he says, "It's not like I don't want to, honest. It just ain't gonn' work right now. Maybe a few months down the road . . ."

A few months! "But the job's here now! It's the one from the sign I saw when I was nearing God, Jackson. You got to come!" Why does he not understand how important this is?

"Look, baby, there ain't nothing I want more'n being back there with you. It's just . . . everyone needs a piece of me lately. I cain't be there for everybody."

"Not even yourself?" I croak.

"'Specially not that," he says. "Get some sleep, girl. I'll call you tomorra."

I hang up and close my eyes. I can't hardly believe it. After all that. I click off the TV. Darkness swallows me up.

I grab Mama's raggedy old cotton throw off the back of the couch and set it over me, then lay back against the cushions. I ain't giving up that easy. I've just got to convince him somehow.

I try to focus on the place where my special feelings come from, to see if I can't figure out where this all's going to lead. Except as I well know, when I try to aim for one of them feelings, they don't never show. It's like I've got to trick them into coming by pretending I don't care none.

Maybe if I were to call his mama and explain it all to her, she'd understand. I could even tell her about the pictures he painted down in his cousins' basement. Then she'd see.

I don't reckon Jackson would appreciate me being that much of a busybody. But it'd be for his own good—okay, yes, mine, too, but still.

Yawning, I decide to sleep here on the couch tonight. Least I won't have to listen to Dog's snoring.

As I'm drifting off to sleep, you know that place before you fully drop off, where you're always dreaming about falling off the curb or off a ledge or what have you, well, it's there that an image comes to me—my daddy stomping off out the door, just exactly how he looked the day he left us. He never turned back that day. But now he does. He looks right at me. His face is all angry and hateful, and then it shifts and reforms itself and it's Jackson's face looking back at me, as he turns and slams the door behind him.

17

*M*ama wakes me up on the couch early the next morning. "What are you doing out here?" she snaps.

I turn over, facing away from her. "Dog was snoring," I say, figuring that's easier than explaining the whole story.

"Go on and sleep in my room, then."

I'm too tired to move.

"You get ahold of Jackson last night?"

"Ungh," I grunt.

"Well?" she says, wanting to hear how it went, as she rushes about getting ready for work.

I pull the blanket over my head.

"That bad, huh?"

I don't dignify her question with an answer.

"Look, baby, I know you got a bee in your bonnet about getting him to move back here, but I think you just gonn' have to accept that he ain't ready to do that right now. May as well go on and learn this one." She sits down beside me and pulls the throw off my head. "When you love somebody, you got to set 'em free. If they love you, they'll come back."

"Daddy didn't come back," I whisper.

"No, he didn't," she says real quiet. "And maybe that was for the best."

I can't hide my surprise at hearing her say that. "For the best? Then why are you always moping about him being gone?"

She sighs real heavy. "Don't go thinking you understand my life. Sometimes things just don't turn out the way you expect. I get down about stuff is all. Sure, I miss the man I loved from time to time, but it ain't just him I'm hurting over. I'm always struggling to stay afloat, what with bills and parenting on my own. But that's none of your concern. Now, promise me you gonn' forget about that painting job and do something fun today. Call up Stef or Joie and have a little get-together, whatever you need to do. Dog's getting picked up by Gina, so you got the whole day to yourself." With that, she taps me on the behind, grabs her keys, and blows out the door.

I decide to take Mama's advice and call Stef. She's all weird 'cause I've been grumpy with her ever since that day she got back from camp and couldn't shut up about Jimmy. I don't get how she can't understand that I've had a lot going on. But she agrees to come over and to call Joie as well.

After cleaning up a little, I sit down at the table with my SAT book to wait for them.

I try to be polite as the girls shoot the shit about what all they've been up to this summer. Here they are my very best friends, and I can't help but feel bored. I used to love having them over to talk. But now, it just seems like a chore. Me and Stef are sitting on my bed, and Joie is over on Dog's. Stef keeps pulling on one clump of her straight blond hair while she goes on and on about Jimmy. Joie ain't even had a boyfriend yet. I reckon she's feeling left out, 'cause she's bouncing her skinny butt around on Dog's bed, going on about her cute boy cousin she saw on her family trip to Florida! Ew! Good Lord, they're *related*. What is wrong with that girl?

I try my best to join in. "One day me and Jackson were down at the beach kissing, and Mr. Howard came up and started hinting he might go tell Mama."

"No!" Stef laughs. "Did he tell her?"

"I don't believe so. Mama never did say anything about it."

"Y'all think after I have braces guys'll like me more?" Joie asks.

I can't help but feel sorry for her with them buck teeth. I don't hardly notice them all that much anymore, but I reckon the guys do. Her dad keeps promising to save up for an orthodontist, but it hasn't happened as of yet.

"Come on, now," I say. "You're beautiful just like you are." It's true in the sense that she'd be pretty if it weren't for her teeth.

"Right," she huffs.

I elbow Stef.

"You know you've got the best hair of any of us," she says.

Joie fluffs up her curls, nearly smiling.

"I guarantee you'll have a boyfriend 'fore the summer is out," I say, though I don't necessarily believe it.

"You think so?" she asks.

"I'm sure of it."

"Hell yeah," Stef agrees.

"Thanks, y'all. Go on then, tell us about Jackson."

"He's just so sweet. He came all the way to the hospital in Wilmington when I got sick and stayed right by my side every minute."

"That's just like Jimmy," Stef interrupts. "This one time I had to go to the infirmary with a stomachache, and he came to visit me."

Oh, sure, that's exactly the same thing as driving to Wilmington at five a.m. I bite my tongue and try to be nice.

"How long were y'all together?" I ask.

"I liked him since the first week. And you know me, I wasn't shy about it. But we didn't actually get together until the last three days," Stef says.

Three days! She's been making it sound like they spent every minute together all summer.

"Why did it take so long?" I ask her.

"He kind of had this other girlfriend at first. But I just showed him how I'm way more fun, then he dropped her like a burnt biscuit." She laughs out loud.

"Girl, you are crazy," Joie says, giggling, too.

Stef is just a burr in my side today, trying to compare her little dinky crush to my full-on relationship with a practically grown man, as if they were the same thing. It's ridiculous. She shows us the picture of Jimmy she's got in her wallet, and he's just a shrimpy little kid. Maybe inviting them over wasn't such a bright idea.

"I'm hot. Let's go to the beach," I suggest. They agree, and we go out on our bikes. Then, halfway there, I say, "You know, I ain't feeling so good. I believe the humidity and all the pollen must be messing with my asthma."

"You okay?" Joie asks, looking worried.

"I'll be fine. I probably just need to lay down awhile."

Stef's giving me a funny look, though. I ain't at all sure she's buying it. But I turn back home anyhow. I feel downright awful, tricking them like that. What has gotten into me? They're probably good and pissed, but least now I can be alone. Besides, Jackson said he'd call today, and I don't want to miss that.

When Mama gets home from work, she finds me laid out on the couch flipping channels, two empty bags of microwave buttered popcorn on the floor along with a two-liter bottle of Diet Coke and my forgotten SAT book.

"Good Lord, Savannah! You been laying on that couch all day?"

"Uh-uh. Stef and Joie came over earlier. We even went out."

"Where'd y'all go?" she asks, her hands on her hips like she doesn't believe me. Damn.

"Well . . . we were heading to the beach, but I wasn't feeling good, so I came back home."

"You weren't feeling well? What's wrong? Have you been taking your medicine? Savannah, turn off that television and answer me."

"Yes, I've been taking it every day." I click off the TV. "It wasn't asthma. I just didn't feel good."

"As in you were about to throw up or as in you wanted to come home and wait around for Jackson to call?"

I look up like I'm thinking real hard. "It'd have to be that last one you said, I reckon."

She takes a big, deep breath. "Looky here. I know I haven't exactly set the best example for you. But you gonn' have to pull yourself up and get over this. It ain't like y'all were married. You've only been together a few weeks. This is not the end of the world. It's just the end of one of what will be many crushes you're gonn' have."

She done hit a raw nerve now. I jump up off the couch. "It ain't a crush! Don't you call it that! We may not have spent our whole lives together, but what we got is real. Jackson loves me and it is *not* over, so quit saying that. You're just lonely and pathetic and you want me to be the same, but I'm not, so just leave me alone!" I run to my room and slam the door as hard as I can. I'm shaking from head to toe. Damn, that was mean. I didn't intend to be so ugly.

I hear the front door open and close and the car start. That ain't a good sign. It'd be better if she came in here yelling about respect and punishment. I am up a serious creek.

I promised myself I wasn't going to call Jackson again until he called me like he said he would. But this situation here calls for drastic measures. I dial his number, which my fingers can do all on their own without my brain pitching in at all.

"Hello?" his mama says. Her voice always sounds so pinched and tight, like she's got a stick up her butt.

For a flash of a second, I think about telling her about Jackson's painting, but I hold my tongue. "May I speak to Jackson, please?" I ask all polite.

"Young lady, Jack needs to get on with living a life in Greenville. These phone calls are not helping."

I'm struck dumb, and I feel my temper roiling. But while I'm fuming, trying to find my tongue, she's apparently passing the phone along anyhow. Just as I'm fixing to spill my fury, I hear Jackson's soothing voice.

"Hey, baby," he says, and damn, but I just melt into tears, bawling my dang head off. "Don't worry about her. She don't know what I need. What's wrong?"

"Everything," I squawk.

"Cain't be all that bad," he murmurs.

I want to tell him I'm all tore up inside, that I can't stand that he left, that I can't handle him not calling me when he says he will, that life just pure T sucks without him and I don't care about nothing else, that I want him to realize how important it is that he take that painting job, that I don't care about anything or anybody anymore, 'cause all I can think about is him.

But I know I can't say all that. I know he doesn't want to hear it. And that makes it hurt all the more. So I just keep bawling. And he hangs in there with me, saying things like "I'm here" and "It's okay."

Finally, when I've calmed down, I tell him about the fight I had with Mama. "I said some wicked terrible things. She ain't never gonn' forgive me. And I'm scared what's gonn' happen when she gets home." I start bawling again.

"I wish I could be there, help you straighten this all out." He takes a big, deep breath. "I used to fight with my dad sometimes. Seem to me he appreciated it when I owned up to my mistakes and said sorry first."

I'm happy to hear him opening up about his daddy. But I don't think sorry is going to cut it here.

"Look, I got to go," he says.

"Jackson." I want to ask him why he didn't call like he said he would, when he's going to come visit, what I'm supposed to do without him. But I don't want to be a nag, one more leech on his energy. So I don't say anything at all.

"It's gonn' be okay, girl. You hang in there." And then he clicks off, which bugs the hell out of me. I reckon he doesn't like good-byes. And then I come to realize he hasn't said he loved me but that one time on the beach right before he left. *Does* he love me? *Does* he wish he was here? Or is he just saying it? If he really wanted to be here, wouldn't he be?

There ain't no use letting my mind wander off into that kind of dangerous territory. So I just close the door to those thoughts and get to work on what I can deal with, which is figuring out what to do about Mama. I reckon writing her a note might be the best solution. That way I don't actually got to go look her in her hurt eyes.

I pull out my clipboard and some notebook paper.

Dear Mama,

>*I'm awful sorry for what I said. I didn't mean it. I feel just terrible about it. You're not those things I said. I was just being hateful. And I sure do regret it. I hope you can find it in your heart to forgive me. I reckon my punishment ought to be dishes and laundry for a week. I am truly sorry.*

Love you,
Savannah

I believe that part about the punishment was a good idea, makes it seem like I put some real thought into it *and* gets her mind off restricting phone calls with Jackson instead. I set the note on the kitchen counter where she's likely to see it when she gets home. Then I hide out in my room, so I don't have to face her. Time ticks by real slow. I write all my feelings down in my journal, then pick up my current romance novel, *Pirate of Paradise,* but somehow I just can't get into it. I keep looking at the clock. It sure is quiet. The crickets and the wind are about all I hear, not hardly even any cars going by.

I must have drifted off, 'cause when Mama's car pulls up, the clock shows it's 1:30 a.m. I've been having strange dreams, none too peaceful. I sit up to listen. She's giggling all weird and saying "Shh." I wonder if Gina's with her. But that'd mean that Dog and Dave are alone at Gina's house, and that doesn't seem likely. Something crashes in the kitchen. I jump up and run out into the living room.

"Oopsies," she giggles, a glass shattered across the counter in front of her. She is drunk as a skunk. And there is a man with her! Mama ain't never brought a man home, not ever. This one looks all greasy and creepy. His hair's too long, and so are his beard and mustache.

"Mama," I say, all tentative.

She busts out laughing. Then she sees my note. "Look, Rick, my baby done wrote me a letter. Ain't that sweet?" She picks it up, shaking bits of glass off it. Then she reads it out loud.

"Mama, don't," I say. But she ain't listening. She's embarrassing me, and herself. She's reading it word by word like she's in the third grade.

"She loves me. Awww. What do you think, Rich? A week of dishes and laundry sound like the right price for insulting your mama? Sounds pretty light to me."

"I thought you said it was Rick," I say, though I don't know why I care.

Meanwhile, poor, scummy Rick/Rich is looking back and forth between the two of us like he doesn't know what to do.

Mama hears my words and slowly looks back up at him as if she's realizing she doesn't know who he is, and starts to cry.

"Now, now, ladies," he says. "Ain't no reason why this needs to turn south. You just go on back to bed, little miss. Your mama and I just gonn' have a bit of grown-up time."

Aw! That is disgusting! Mama can't seriously be considering doing you-know-what with the likes of this dude. He don't even look clean. Uh-uh. No way. Not because of something I said. I ain't having it.

Except I ain't got a clue how to get rid of him. Then it hits me. I start rasping and wheezing all the sudden like I'm about to die. Of course Mama knows I ain't having no asthma attack 'cause of the way I'm hamming it up to the hilt. Lordy, I'm pulling it out full on, sounding near about like a donkey. I pretend to take a hit off my inhaler.

Suddenly, Rick looks like he's about to be hauled off by the police. He don't want no part of anything messy. "What's wrong with her?" he asks, staring at me like I'm some sort of mental defective.

Mama meets my eyes. Then she turns to Rick, really looks at him, then smiles back at me. "She's sick. I'ma have to take her to Wilmington. You want to drive us? The emergency room ain't that bad this time of night."

His eyes bug out of his head.

"No? I believe I've had too much to drink to drive out all that way, but I can call a girlfriend," Mama says.

I love that she's playing along, so I get even more dramatic, falling down on the couch, clutching my throat, until Rick hightails it out the door, and Mama and I bust out in giggles.

We laugh until our sides hurt. Then I get her some Advil and put on a pot of coffee. It's been a long time since Mama came home drunk. She used to do it more often when she and Gina were newly abandoned, but that was years ago. I still remember, though, they'd always take Advil and drink coffee. I clean up the broken glass while the coffee's brewing, then pour Mama a cup and add two sugars and milk till it's white. I set it on the coffee table in the living room and plop myself down right beside her.

"I really am sorry," I whisper, feeling like I might cry again.

She turns to me and strokes my hair. "It never happened," she says. I give her a big hug for that one. "Go on to bed."

"Mama," I say, getting up to obey, "you set me a better example than you think. You showed me that true love is what it's all about and that the likes of Rick over there ain't even worth the trouble."

Her eyes fill up with tears and feeling. She doesn't need to say anything, though. I understand. I turn back to my room, knowing now I can sleep in peace.

18

Something sure did shift after the Rick incident. Me and Mama are getting along better than we have in a long while. She's even talking about saving up some money to build on an extra room, so me and Dog don't got to share no more. Somehow, I seem to be getting used to the idea that Jackson is staying in Greenville. I don't like it one bit, mind you, but I guess you could say I'm tolerating it.

It was seriously embarrassing having to call the guy at the construction site, telling him Jackson wouldn't be able to take the job after all. Not only did it make me sad as hell to say them words out loud, but the dude laid into me, thinking I'd pulled some kind of prank on him, hollering about how falsifying documents is a felony offense and whatnot. He said if I show my face around there again, he'll call the cops!

I wanted to tell him to quit taking himself so seriously and to have a little sympathy for a girl whose heart was breaking. But instead I just suggested Jackson might be available at some point down the line and that I didn't mean no harm.

On my way to work, I stop by the junior college and find the Living Through Literature group. I listen in at the back awhile. Today they're discussing *Great Expectations* by Charles Dickens. As much as I love to read, what I ain't too keen on is the way teachers insist on picking at the natural beauty of a story, tearing it up to see what meaning might be hidden, which seems to be exactly what they're doing today. Maybe it's for the best I didn't join their program. I bet it would have driven me crazy.

I slip back out of the auditorium and still have some time to spare. As I wander around the campus, I notice the art gallery and poke my head in.

"Need something?" a man arranging some pottery asks me. He's got Albert Einstein hair and granny glasses perched on the end of his nose. His bright yellow smock stands out even in a room so full of color.

"No, thank you," I reply, heading back out.

"Look around. Take it in," he says, waving his arms around the room, then letting them come to rest on his belly.

So I stay and admire all the different types of artwork—pots and sculptures and drawings and paintings.

"You an artiste?" he asks me.

I look right into his deep brown eyes. He looks kind. "No," I say, "but I have a friend who paints beautiful pictures. He's out of high school already and works at a body shop. But he's very talented."

I don't know why I spill my guts like this. I reckon it's something to do with missing out on that Living Through Literature program—even if it might have irritated me—and not wanting Jackson to miss out on possibilities, too.

"Talented, huh?" He scratches his head under all that hair. "Tell your friend to come on by, bring in some of his paintings for me to peruse."

"Really?" I ask.

"Absotively. I'm always interested in meeting *talented* young people." He winks like maybe he doesn't believe me about Jackson's abilities.

"Thank you, sir," I say, anyhow. "I'll tell him."

It's my day to read to the little kids at the library. It turns out to be one of the good times. A bunch of adorable, drooly toddlers sit on their mothers' laps, their sweet smiles as big as if it were Christmas. Something about being around their joyful spirits brings mine up a notch. After the kids disperse to look for books to check out, I slip into the computer area and go online. I look up the Blue Ridge Mountains and the University of North Carolina, Asheville. Then I search for information about that program for high-school students. It looks real cool, like a sneak peek at college. They have all these different tracks to choose from for your semester courses, like political science and pre-med. They even have journalism and creative writing! I wish there was some way for me to try to get myself into it. But all you can do is wait and see if you get accepted. With little likelihood of Jackson returning anytime soon, I may as well find me some way to get out of this town, where everything reminds me of how much I miss him.

I go find a copy of *Great Expectations* and check it out. I haven't had to read that one for school yet, and I have to admit, I'm curious. Taking a quick look, I find that it ain't at all easy to read. I'll have to switch back and forth between it and maybe a good Danielle Steele novel, just so my brain doesn't rebel against having to work so hard in summertime.

When I get home after work, I call Jackson, anxious to tell him about the art guy.

"Hey, it's me," I say.

"Me, who?" he asks.

"Jackson?"

"Tyler," he says.

"Oh." I can't hide my disappointment. "Is Jackson there?"

"He's working."

"Can you please tell him Savannah called?"

"Savannah?" he says. "You the one from the beach?"

"Yeah," I reply, not sure if I'm pleased he's heard my name or distressed by the way he put that statement. "When will he be back?"

"I don't know. I'll tell him you called," he says, and hangs up, just like his brother. Didn't anybody ever teach those boys to say bye first?

Stef and Joie invited me to the movies tonight. I reckon I'll go, even if it will mean an entire evening of listening to all the "hilarious" things Jimmy said at camp.

Mama is so excited I'm actually going out, she's acting like I'm going to the prom or something.

"Maybe we could get you something special to wear before you go," she says.

"Mama, I'm going to the movies. With Stef and Joie. Why would I need something special to wear? Shorts and a T-shirt and flip-flops will do me just fine." Sheesh. What is her deal lately?

"Ain't nothing wrong with looking your best. You never know . . ."

"You never know *what*?"

"I'm just saying."

"Saying what exactly?" I ask, starting to feel like this plan might just suck something fierce. "Do you know something I don't?"

She shrugs—not a good sign.

"Spill it." Now she's trying to act all busy in the kitchen, when we both know perfectly well there ain't a thing in there needs doing. "Fine, then," I say, sitting down on the couch, "I ain't going."

That sure gets her attention. "Oh, yes you are, if I got to tote you there myself. You are going. You are not going to set around here moping one more night, not one more. Do you hear me?"

"Then you tell me what all this is about. Why are you suddenly so concerned about what I'm wearing? If y'all are planning something I can't know about, then I don't want no part of it." Besides, I'm thinking, Jackson could call while I'm out, and who knows if I'd be able to reach him back.

Mama sighs and parks her butt beside mine. "Looky here, darlin'. It ain't like it's some big conspiracy. I reckon Joie was sick to death of hearing y'all going on and on about Jackson and Jimmy all the time, so she came up with the idea to get together with some local boys, you know, so y'all can all have fun together, like you used to."

"I know Joie is real desperate to find a boyfriend, but that don't mean I'm gonn' go out on a blind date just for that."

"It ain't a blind date," Mama lies, 'cause now it's all clear as day. "Her mama said—"

"How could she not at least tell me what she had planned? You have to admit that is just pitiful rude. I have got no intention of cheating on Jackson."

"Vannah, please. You can't cheat on someone you're not even with."

Now that was just mean.

"I'm going to bed and I do not want to be disturbed!" I slam the door but good.

Picking up my hairbrush off my dresser, I hold it a moment, then fling it as hard as I can. It whistles its way across the room and lands with a satisfying *thwack* against the wall, leaving a nice black mark on the white paint. Damn, that felt good. I go retrieve it, hold it a minute, then send it sailing back the other way. *Thwack!* Another fine dark bruise on the wall, taking the red hot anger out of my veins. A couple more throws and I'm feeling much better.

Dog comes in acting all surprised by my behavior. "Damn, who licked the red off your candy?"

"Piss off," I growl.

I grab a sweatshirt and march straight through the living room to the front door. "I'm going out," is all I say, knowing it's going to kill Mama all night wondering if I met up with them kids or not. As if!

I ride my bike straight to the 7-Eleven to use the pay phone. I've got to find out if Stef knew about tonight's secret agenda. She about keels over when I tell her what Joie had planned.

"She was trying to get us to cheat on our boyfriends so she could get one?" Stef yells. "Of all the low-down, two-faced, scheming . . ."

Suddenly I feel like we're a team and it doesn't even matter if Jimmy's just a dumb little kid. It dawns on me that it's possible Stef is the only person that may have some notion of what I'm feeling.

"Hell. Meet me at the theater. We'll go see a different movie, just the two of us," Stef suggests.

"What about Joie? We can't just ditch her with all them guys." I am pissed, but that's downright cold.

"I got to think on that one," she says. "I'll take care of Joie. Just meet me at the movies."

I wait for Stef, hoping we don't run into Joie. That would just be too much, having to stand her up to her face. Maybe we should have gone somewhere else. It must be hard for Joie, her two best friends being in relationships, even if the guys don't live here, I think, as I watch all the couples heading into the theater. It seems like near about everybody is half of a pair these days. Everywhere I go it's just couples, couples, couples. Most of them are making out right there in public. They could at least wait until they get inside and the lights dim.

Stef comes marching up, looking agitated. "I done told her we was both canceling out. She was madder than a wet hen in a tote sack, too."

"Bless her heart, but she done brung it on herself," I say. "If she'd at least told us what she was planning, maybe we could have worked something out. But that right there was just deceitful."

"Let's go watch us a movie and forget about these durn people trying to run our lives," Stef says.

And for the first time all summer, she is finally making some sense.

19

We're shelling peas for supper when Mama says, "Hon, I know you're all mad about Joie's plan the other day, but it just ain't right for you to put all your eggs in one basket."

I do not want to get into this with her right now. "I'ma have to make that choice for myself," I say, hoping she gets the point.

"I'm just saying, you can't exactly expect a grown man to wait on a young'un like yourself when y'all live at such a great distance. I'm sure Jackson's got other girls interested in him over there in Greenville."

Anger, like a tornado, tears right through my chest. "Why are you saying this to me?" I cry, throwing the peas down on the kitchen table. "Jackson ain't like that."

"You may not think so, shug, but men just are not to be relied upon. Look what happened with your daddy; he walked away from his family and never looked back. Trust me, I understand these things better'n you think."

"You *don't* understand! You think you do, but you don't. Jackson ain't nothing like Daddy, so don't even try to compare 'em!"

"Men are all the same, darlin'. They are always gonn' let you down."

"That may be true for you. But it ain't gonn' be for me."

Mama laughs. She actually laughs like I'm some dumb kid that just doesn't get it, and damn but that burns me up. And suddenly her face looks so hateful, I can't hold back.

"Maybe you have rotten taste in men," I say, and I know I am pissing her off on purpose.

"You best watch your mouth, there," she says. And I can see she's steaming.

"You done spent the last twelve years pining over him and he didn't deserve but one minute of it. He was a no-count, good-for-nothing . . ." My words stop as I feel the sting of her hand across my face. Mama looks about as stunned as I am.

All these years she ain't never laid a hand on neither one of us, and now she goes and does it—over him?

"Yeah," I say, biting back my tears. "That's just what I saw the day he left."

An image has just crashed its way into my head that I've been trying to blot out as long as I can remember. It takes up all the space in my brain and spills right out my mouth. "Y'all thought I was napping like Dog, but I wadn't. I heard the loud voices." And now it's as fresh in my mind as the slap stinging on my cheek. "I crept down the hall and peeked in through the keyhole. Y'all were arguing, which wadn't anything new. I saw you trying to unpack the suitcase he was packing. You picked up a blue shirt, turned to put it back in the closet. You were yelling about how the young'uns needed him, and he wouldn't take it no more. I seen that click in his eyes, that moment when he'd just had it and he hauled off and hit you but good."

Mama gasps as if she's been struck, grasping her face. "You couldn't possibly remember that," she whispers. "You weren't but three years old."

"Some things leave their mark," I say. "I couldn't believe he'd done that. Not my daddy. I drew in my breath, and you turned as if you'd heard me. And I saw his big ol' nasty fist print on your face. And I started hollering, just hollering my dang head off. I don't even know why or what I thought it would do." I am positively bawling at this point. But the floodgates are open and there ain't no stopping now. "He came stomping out the room, and I thought he was gonn' hit me, too. And I kept right on screaming. And he ran out without even looking my way." I stop to catch my breath, remembering how Mama picked me up then to quiet my tears.

"Stop," Mama whimpers, "just quit."

"Jackson ain't one bit like him." Though for the tiniest of moments the image of Jackson punching his cousin in the face pops into my mind. I remind myself that was to defend me and send that old image on its way. I turn and stomp out the front door just exactly like my daddy did all them years ago.

I ride my bike hard and fast, tearing down the street like a cat from a coyote, hoping to God I know what I'm talking about. Of course I do. Jackson *is* different. I just know he is. Please, dear Lord, don't let me be wrong on this one. I ride until I find myself out past that construction site, past that trailer. My sign is gone, but them rocks are still down there in the sand. I set down my bike and climb on up, panting like a dog. I've just got to catch my breath, that's all. I'm shaking from head to toe, can't even believe the things that just came out of my mouth. What is wrong with me lately? Treating my friends like crap, hurting Mama like that, this just ain't like me at all. And now I went and wore out my lungs. And fool that I am, I ain't got my inhaler. I left the house in such a tizzy, I didn't stop to think. I've just got to calm down is all, 'cause this here situation is bad. My chest is all closed up. I'm wheezing like crazy, miles from home, nobody likely to go looking for me anytime soon and certainly not way out here. Good Lord, Savannah, you've gone and done it now.

I slither down the rocks to my bike, pick it up and wheel it back out to the street. I ain't got a choice. I'm going to have to ride myself over to Mercy. I'll just have to go real slow is all. But things are looking kind of wavery. I'm seeing some sort of black spots in the air. Suddenly, one of my strange feelings comes over me. It don't make much sense given how bad off I am at the moment. 'Cause what comes is the notion of good times on the way, a sense of excitement and adventure.

"You all right there?" a voice calls.

I try to focus on the figure in the distance. It all seems like shadows, but then I see that guy with the caterpillar mustache standing out on the steps of the trailer, the one who threatened to call the cops on me when Jackson couldn't take that painting gig. He's leaning on the railing out front, a cigar blowing smoke in his face.

"I remember you," he says, pointing at me, and he sounds none too happy.

I give up the goat, quit fighting to plow forward through what feels like molasses, and let myself drop to the ground. Only somehow, I manage to whack my head on a lamppost on the way, and next thing I know, I'm slipping into darkness.

20

There's a sweetness in the air—a fresh sort of springy crispness. Not a lick of humidity. The grass is as soft and green as the day it first came up out of the ground. There's little colorful flowers everywhere and the trees look practically like they sprung up out of a storybook—just perfect for a tire swing or a tree house. Jackson's standing right under one of them, a big ol' grin on his face. And as I look around, I realize we're back at the church picnic. Everybody looks sort of different, though, and Mama's nowhere to be seen.

I simply glide on over to Jackson. He takes me into his arms like I've been dreaming about for so long. And Stef's there and she can plainly see that this is way bigger than her little ol' crush on Jimmy.

The cool air breezes across my face. My chest feels clear as day. I'm breathing so good, my lungs feel ten times their usual size. Jackson's smiling down at me, and his face is moving ever so slow toward mine. But then we hear a siren positively blaring like it's right on top of us. I wish it would shut on up so we can get back to what we were about to do. But then there's a dag light glaring in my eyes, giving me a headache, it's so bright.

"Come on, little lady, hang in there," says a vaguely familiar voice. I wish it would go away so I could get back to where I was at. But I take a peek, and that grouchy guy with the mustache from the construction site by the HOUSEPAINTERS NEEDED sign is looking down at me, and beside him is some other fella in a white uniform, and come to find out we're bouncing around in the back of an ambulance!

My head is blaring with pain. I try to ask them what on God's green earth is going on, but they can't hardly hear me through the oxygen mask.

"I still had your number on file from that bogus application you put in," Caterpillar Mustache says. "Your mama's on her way. She'll meet us at the hospital and your bike's safe inside my trailer. You're lucky I come out for a smoke when I did, I tell you what."

Well doesn't he have all the answers? Now if he could quit his yammering so's I could find my way back to wherever I was at, I sure would be grateful. Ah hell, I just realized, it was all some kind of dream. I wasn't with Jackson at all. It seemed so real. Now that's about the saddest news I done ever heard.

This hospitalization ain't at all like the last one. For one thing, Mercy is old and run-down, and the head honcho doctor is that mean old baldy guy who insists on blaming me for having this dang asthma. For another, Mama seems to have changed sides of the court, jumping on the bandwagon of blaming me for riding off in a huff and not bringing my inhaler. And to top it all off, Jackson's too busy working to trouble himself with coming down to check up on me.

In the two days I've been in this Godforsaken hole, I've had exactly three visitors. Dog was bored silly, saying, "How do you stand it in here?" as if I had a choice. Meanwhile, he gets to go stay over with his best friend. Gina came with him, but she doesn't really count since she was here to see Mama. Dave waited down in the lobby the whole time. He doesn't like hospitals. Then there was Stef, who would not shut up about Jimmy the Great, because, Lord save us all, he is coming out here next weekend with his Bible group. And finally, Mr. Caterpillar Mustache! Now why in the world would he want to come visit? Says he feels responsible since he helped rescue me. I told him I don't need another daddy thank you very much. Mama went and scolded me for being rude. And now, grosser than gross, he is getting all flirtatious with her. Can we please remember this is a hospital, as in with sick people in it? Lord, sometimes folks just ain't got no respect. Besides, she needs to be worrying about how to keep her job at Harris Teeter, not turning on the charm for some *old* guy.

Out of sheer boredom, I call Joie. "What's up?" I say, aiming to show her all is forgotten.

"Why are you calling me?" she asks, rather rudely.

"I'm in the hospital," I say, thinking that might cause her to calm her tone.

"I heard," she replies coldly.

"Thanks for checking up on me." I laugh.

She's silent.

"What are *you* mad for?" I ask. "You're the one that tried to trick us." Now I'm getting pissed again.

"I have to go," she says. "My *true* friends are meeting me at the beach."

"*True* friends?" Now what is that supposed to mean?

"Bye," she says.

I'm telling you, this hospital has got some bad juju.

Mama rouses me from a nap to tell me Jackson's on the phone. He's been calling me every day since I got here. He promised he's going to come down to visit on the weekend sometime real soon. My head hurts so bad from where I knocked it on the lamppost, even him calling can't cheer me up. I've got a bruise the size of Texas back there. I'm lonely, bored, and rightly sick to death of this place.

"Hey," I say, sounding as pathetic as I feel.

"Y'okay?" he asks.

And suddenly, without even putting any thought to it, I say, "Tell me the truth, Jackson, would you ruther be done with me?"

He's dead quiet at first, scaring the bejesus out of me. But then he turns all serious and says, "Ain't nut'n changed on my end of things. That how you feel?" And his voice sounds all hurt and tight.

"Me? Are you kidding? Lord, Jackson, I'd give my right arm just to see you for ten whole minutes!"

He laughs and tells me I done scared the pants off him. I feel so relieved, my mood finally brightens. And even though it took me getting all melancholy to get to where I could ask him that question, I sure am glad I did.

"By the way," I say, "I've been meaning to tell you, I went by the art gallery at the junior college one day and I told the guy there about your paintings and he said he'd really like it if you'd bring some by for him to take a look at."

He's real quiet. "Why?" he finally says.

"Why *what*?"

"Why should I bring 'em over there?"

"I don't know. He said he's always interested in meeting talented young people."

"What good will it do me?" He sounds nearly angry.

"It's a connection," I say. "You never know."

"Hm," is all he says. Then back to the usual, "I got to run."

Oh well, at least we cleared up the heavy-duty question. I believe Mama nearly had me convinced that he was through with me, had me imagining him out there in Greenville dating all sorts of girls. Shoot. Maybe now she's got a man interested in her (even if he does look old and scummy), she'll lay off of dumping on Jackson.

Speak of the devil, here comes Mr. Caterpillar Mustache for yet another visit, stinking to high heaven of cigars and Aqua Velva. I understand he helped get me an ambulance when I needed it. But he ain't fooling nobody. The way he's drooling all over Mama, wouldn't nobody believe he's here to check up on me. Mama *is* pretty. I've always known it. But salivating over her right beside her daughter's hospital bed seems to me to be in bad taste.

"Hey there, Savannah," he says, his eyes on Mama. "Miss Porsha," he says softly, bowing slightly.

"Hello again," Mama says, looking a mite irritated by his presence.

I've got to hide my smile on that, not like anybody's looking.

"Thought maybe I could take you out for a walk, get some fresh air," he says to Mama. "If that's a'ight with you," he asks me.

Like I care. Least it'll get Mama out of my hair for a spell. Having her around every minute of every day usually means she ends up riding on my nerves.

Mama gives me a slight shake of her head like she's wanting me to say no. But I ain't in the mood for games.

I shrug. "Y'all go on ahead," I say.

"You want to come with?" she asks me.

I hate walking around attached to the IV pole. "I'm tired," I say, laying my head down like I'm fixing to go to sleep.

Mama looks pissed. But I know she won't turn him down, she owes him that much, and truth be told, she could use some fresh air.

Soon as she goes, the nurse comes in for my next nebulizer treatment, which I'm getting awful sick of, thank you very much. After she finishes, I flip channels on the TV, feeling sort of sorry for myself. Least I ain't half as bad as the crazy folks what air out all their dirty laundry on daytime television. What in the world can they be thinking?

Jackson calls back, rescuing me from my boredom.

"Guess what?" he says.

"What?" I ask, hoping maybe he's coming to visit.

"My Aunt June just called."

"How come?" I ask.

"Billy Jo and Junior got into a knock-down drag-out over some girl they both liked. While their parents was pulling them off each other, Junior got so mad, he told 'em how Billy Jo brought that punch in the nose from me all on hisself, goading me by calling you names and such."

"Are you serious?"

"Sure am. Then, get this, he said the whole party was Billy Jo's idea, not mine, and Billy Jo said it was Junior's. Their parents got so mad, they took away the boys' truck for a month and grounded 'em both."

"Holy cow!"

"My aunt said she was calling to tell me they were sorry for blaming me and kicking me out and all."

"That's amazing. I reckon you were right about giving 'em some time. You sure are smart."

"I'm just relieved we put this to rest," he says. "I hate having people mad at me."

"Maybe now you can come down for a visit," I suggest.

"Maybe," he says. Then he gets real quiet.

"You okay?" I ask him.

"There's sump'n else I need to tell you. I wadn't sure if it was a good idea when we talked earlier on, but I think being truthful is the right way to go."

I swallow hard, wondering what in the world he could be talking about.

"I went out with somebody the night before you ended up back in the hospital."

"Whatcha mean by somebody?" I ask.

"Like a girl," he says, "but listen, now, 'fore you get upset, it's good news."

"Good news?" I cry. "Since when is being cheated on good news?" And my brain rushes into all kinds of terrible thoughts about Mama being right and men being untrustworthy by their very nature and Jackson being just like my daddy.

"It ain't like 'at," he says. "Let me explain. See, Mama kept ridin' on me to go out with other girls. She kept on saying we're too young for a long-distance thing and making a big deal about the difference in our ages. And I just went right on ignorin' her. But then, that night, I came home from work and my old girlfriend was there."

"Your old *girlfriend*?" I believe I'm about to have a seizure.

"We used to go out 'fore I met you, but we split up right before my dad died. Anyhow, like I was saying, Mary Elizabeth was there at the house."

"*Mary Elizabeth*?" I whine. Somehow that name conjures up images in my mind of the perfect little woman, not just a kid like me. Needless to say, I pale in comparison.

"I ain't sure if Mama invited her or if she just showed up. But at that point my choices were to set with her and my ma all evening or to take her out."

"You could have said no," I whimper.

"You're missing the point, girl. I did it like an experiment. And see, what I found out was, well, what I feel for you is sump'n special."

"You didn't already know that?"

"I did. But Mama had me all mixed up. It was like I had to prove it to myself. So I'd know once and for all she was wrong."

"And just how did you do that?"

"At the end of the night, when I kissed Mary Elizabeth good-bye—"

"You *kissed* her?"

"Wait, now. Listen. It was a good-bye kiss, 'cause I told her I wadn't interested. And the thing I'm trying to tell you is 'at it was like kissing a sister or an aunt. I didn't feel nothin'. So you see, it made me get it how what we got is special."

The thought of him kissing somebody else is just too much. "I believe I better go," I say real quiet. Then, for once, it's me that clicks off. I reckon it's for the best he told me now while I'm under medical care. You see what I mean about bad juju?

I must have cried myself to sleep, 'cause I wake up when I hear Mama coming back in the room. Lord, it's nearly dark out!

"That's a lot of fresh air," I snap. What if I'd needed her? What if the doctors had wanted to do something more than my regular treatments and she wasn't there? She never leaves me alone so long in the hospital.

"You said you needed to sleep. I didn't want to disturb you," she explains.

But something about the way she's trying to look busy folding clothes tells me that right there is a fib. Somehow that old goat has caught her attention. Yuck!

"You actually like him?" I ask.

"He's friendly enough," Mama replies.

"Oh, yeah, he's a real peach," I say, thinking back on how he threatened me with calling the cops. "If you're okay with leaving me alone so long, maybe you ought to get on back to work."

"Now, Van, a couple of hours is different than being gone all day.

Besides, I told the nurses where they could find me if anything came up."

"You'll lose your job again," I fret. "Just explain it to your boss. He'll understand."

"He'll have to trust me without explanations. I ain't opening the door to nobody's pity. Now why are you looking so forlorn?" she asks.

"No reason," I say. "No reason a-tall."

The next afternoon, I wake up from a nap to hear Mama yelling on the telephone. She is steaming mad. She done lost her job. It's the same every time I get hospitalized. Why wouldn't they fire her if she doesn't show up to work all week and refuses to give any explanations? Here we are trying to talk it through, when who strolls in but Mr. Caterpillar Mustache, handing Mama a lunch bag he brought for her, which I guess is a lucky thing, 'cause she was irritating me earlier, so I didn't share my hospital lunch with her like I usually do.

"Hey, there, Savannah, how you feeling?" he says, all too cheerful.

I give him the stink eye, 'cause frankly, I ain't got time for his shenanigans today. But Mama slaps my thigh, so I smile all fake at him. "Swell," I say.

They don't even notice my tone, 'cause now he's staring all googly-eyed at her and she's blushing and turning away. I'm telling you, it is just disgusting. Can't she see what a slimeball he is? He's smelly and aging poorly. Plus, I can't rightly stand the way he twirls his old caterpillar mustache when he's ogling her.

Lord, does she have bad taste in men! Holy hell, it's going to get worse, because all the sudden, the room starts to swaying around, and the feeling that comes over me is that these two are in it for the long haul. I imagine what Mama might look like in a wedding dress, and she sure would be beautiful, but then I picture him up there with her, his balding, cigar-smoking, caterpillar-mustache self. Ugh! I close my eyes and try to blot out the image.

"No, sir!" I yell right out loud. "I will not have it!" Course they ain't got a clue what I'm hollering about. If she wants to marry someone, couldn't it be some nice young dude her own age, who at least has a full head of hair and doesn't smoke cigars or douse himself in cheap cologne?

"Savannah, where are your manners?" Mama chides, bringing me back to the present.

"Mister, I think you better go. I'm not feeling too well," I say. And then, honest-to-God, I throw up my lunch right there on the bed.

Everybody starts to rushing around. Mama's getting all upset. She's calling the nurses. They're calling the doctor. 'Cause they all know, there ain't no reason for me to be hurling like that, unless something's gone wrong with my meds or whatnot. Mr. Caterpillar Mustache slinks on out the door.

When things settle back down, Mama says, "That was thoughtful of him to bow out when things were getting messy. Prob'ly didn't want to embarrass you."

The calm doesn't last long. 'Cause next thing you know, I'm running to the bathroom and cramping something fierce. Come to find out, the chicken they served for lunch was bad, and half the patients are puking their guts out! Some freaking hospital!

Mama's gloating 'cause Mr. Caterpillar Mustache brought her an egg salad sandwich he made himself. The smell of it sends me into a state of constant stomach contractions.

I wake up drenched in sweat and dizzy. I ain't never felt this bad in my whole entire life. It must be late, 'cause the ward is actually quiet. Mama's sleeping in the recliner, but the TV is showing reruns of *Scrubs*. I still feel like I might throw up, but there ain't nothing left in me to heave. I ought to sue this dang place.

Mama must have heard me stirring, 'cause next thing I know her hand's stroking my hair. "Lord, darlin', you're wet as a dishrag." She gets a warm washcloth and starts sponging my face. But it feels all clammy.

"I wanna go home," I say, and even I'm surprised how weak my voice sounds.

"Soon enough, baby girl," she says. "Jackson called while you were sleeping."

I try to sit up, but my head is swimming. "Why didn't you wake me?" I moan.

She looks kind of stern at me. "You weren't in no condition to talk. He said to tell you he's real sorry and he hopes you feel better soon. You want to tell me what it is he's sorry about?"

"No, ma'am," I reply.

"All right, then," she sighs. "I got some other good news, too."

Jackson's coming to visit! That just has to be it! Lord, I could use a little good news right now. He must want to make it up to me.

"Denny's offered me a job." She's smiling like she's all proud or something.

"Denny's?" I ask. *That's* the good news? "You hate waitressing, Mama. Don't settle for that."

But she starts in to laughing. "Not the restaurant! *Denny!* You know, the man that saved your life?" She looks all shocked that I don't know what she's talking about.

"Mr. Caterpillar Mustache?" I say.

"What? Lord, Savannah, *Denny Johnson*, from the paintin' job."

None of this is making any sense. Mama is going to take the job from the yellow sign that was meant for Jackson? "You gonn' paint houses?"

I don't like that she keeps laughing about everything. Excuse me for being a little confused. I have spent the entire day puking my guts out after being poisoned by the hospital, in case you forgot.

"He offered me a job in the office, you know, filing, typing, secretarial work."

"You ain't qualified for that." I know this, because that's what she's been told every durn time she ever applied for a secretarial position.

Now she looks all huffy, like I insulted her. "He said he'd teach me what I need to know."

"I bet he will," I murmur.

"Now, just what do you mean by that?" she barks.

I'd like to retort, but I ain't got it in me.

"Never mind," she says. "Just think about it, Van, a job where the boss already knows about your asthma. He done promised he wadn't offering out of pity, that he'd excuse my absences when necessary, long as I make up my hours."

Make up the hours, huh? I'm sorry, but my mind is in the gutter on that one.

"Please, baby, be happy for me on this." Her voice sounds pathetic. "We'll even get full health benefits."

"Oh, Mama," I say softly, knowing just how much that means. "That sure is great."

Before I drift off to sleep, I say a silent prayer. "Thank you, Lord, for blessing Mama with a new job with medical coverage, and please, Lord, don't let her marry Denny Caterpillar. Thank you, amen."

21

When we come home from the longest four-day stay in the hospital I've ever had, my bike is waiting for me on the front steps. I reckon Denny Caterpillar brought it by from the construction site. I ain't at all sure how he knows where we stay at, but I'm glad not to have to go fetch it and all. Meanwhile, Mama hasn't said word one about the fight we had before I ran off. Neither has she apologized for slapping me. We sort of stepped right around it and moved on.

No sooner do we get into the house than Stef's on the phone. Before I can even say hello, she's off on a rant about Jimmy the Great. I take the phone to my room and lay down on the bed.

"His Bible group is coming to town tomorra! The preacher is choosing out which visitor stays with which of our church families, and—"

"*Our* church? Since when do you go to church?" I ask, never having known her to attend one.

"Shut up! I been going down every Sundy."

"Since when?"

"Since a couple weeks ago."

"Since you found out his Bible group is coming to town more like."

"So?"

"So the preacher's choosing the families," I say, leading her back to her point.

"I'm just flat out worried he won't place Jimmy with us 'cause I seemed too interested. What'll I do then?"

"You'll just make yourself a friend of whosever house he's at," I say. Duh!

"Vannah, what if y'all sign up," she says, sounding all excited.

"Pardon me?" I ain't ready for some Bible thumper staying over and judging us.

"*Please.* Hardly nobody with kids our age signed up to host. If y'all do it, I'm positive you'd get him."

Oh joy. Just what I need, a weekend of recuperating with Jimmy the Great staying at our house and Stef hanging all over him. Between the inhaler treatments I've got to do, oral steroids making me irritable, and feeling worn out, I just want to be left alone. I've got to stall for time. "I'ma have to check with Mama. She's pretty tired from being at the hospital with me all week and she's starting a new job and . . ." I'm fixing to tell her about the gross flirting going on with Denny Caterpillar, but that ain't ready for public consumption just yet. I'm sort of embarrassed about Mama going after him. She's so pretty and he's so, well . . . old. He looks like he's nearing fifty!

"Please, Vannah, I'll do anything."

"There ain't no guarantee we'll even get Jimmy."

"I know you will. I just know it."

I sigh, feeling stuck as a hog in a bog. "I'll see if I can talk Mama into it."

"You are the best friend ever! I swear I'll return the favor someday," she blubbers.

"I ain't promising anything," I explain, feeling guilty that here I've been such a lousy friend since she got back from camp and she's praising me as if I deserve it.

"Thank you! Thank you! Thank you!" she squeals.

Part of me wishes I could talk to her about what Jackson did with Mary Elizabeth. Stef has always been the one to give me advice about guys. But I'm just too embarrassed, too worried about what it might could mean about me and Jackson's future. Instead, I say bye and hang up.

Least Mama ain't likely to go for Stef's request. I head out to the living room.

"What are you *doing*?" I ask.

"Ironing, what's it look like?" she says, as if she does this every day.

"Since when do you iron?"

"Since I got me a quality job."

Quality? Filing papers for Denny Caterpillar is quality? What is the world coming to?

"You want something or not?" she snaps.

Oh, yeah, Stef. I've got to present this in such a way that it seems like I'm trying (I owe Stef that much), but without actually making it work (I ain't that crazy). Mama has begun whistling a cheerful tune.

"Stef called. Her boyfriend from camp is coming to town with his Bible group. Apparently, our church is looking for families to host the Bible-group folks. And Stef wants to know can we sign up. But don't worry, I know how busy you are getting ready for the new job and you're tired from being at the hospital and all. So, it's okay if—"

"No, honey, that sounds real nice. You go on and sign us up." And she starts in whistling again!

"Pardon me?" She ain't helping with this here plan at all.

"I said okay."

"Why?" Can't she tell a half-assed request when she hears one?

Mama laughs. "I think it's a nice idea."

"We might ought to have to go to church with 'em and all," I warn, praying she'll change her mind.

"That'd be great. I been thinking about getting more active in the church," she says. That iron is zooming across skirt after skirt. I had no idea she had so many.

"Have you gone crazy?" I ask.

Her smile creeps me out. "Denny and I had some time to talk about, well, God and this and that while you were in the hospital and it got me to thinking, is all."

"Just how much time did y'all spend together?" I ask.

She tries to hide a smile. "Aside from the times you saw him come by, he visited a few more when you were resting, called sometimes after you went to sleep at night."

Ugh. I believe she may actually like the dude.

"What?" she asks, perhaps noticing my wrinkled-up nose.

"What can you see in him?" I blurt out.

"Savannah!" she scolds. "He done saved your life. I expect better of you." When I don't say nothing, she adds, "He may not be much to look at, but he's awful kind and real thoughtful, too."

It sure is something hearing her be so positive about a man. I mean, I'm happy for her, but I can't help wishing she'd chosen someone younger and cuter and maybe without a temper that causes him to threaten somebody with calling the cops just for trying to help out a friend.

"It ain't like we're getting married or nothing!"

That image of her in a wedding gown lurks in my mind, making me feel like I may just throw up again.

"He makes me feel like . . . never mind." She goes back to ironing.

"Like what?" I ask, real quiet, wondering what it is she's embarrassed to say.

"He just makes me feel special is all. He brought me food and little gifts to the hospital, took me out, made me laugh. Ain't nobody ever done that in all these years of hospital visits. And there's just something about spending time with a person during those intense moments in life that's . . . different. Listen to me ramblin' on. Anyhow, we had some time talking and he got me thinking about the church and God."

Dog slams in through the front door. "Did I just hear Mama say she been thinking about God? You going through the change or something?"

"Dog! Good night! How old you think I am? Alls I said was, I been thinking about being more active in the church. Wouldn't hurt neither one of y'all to spend a little more time there."

"Looky here," Dog starts, "you going through some kind of life crisis, you go right on ahead. But you leave me out of it."

Mama turns all red and blotchy. "Don't you dare be disrespectful to me! I done raised you and fed and clothed you! I expect better than that, young man! You go on to your room and you can just stay there until supper!"

"What the hell?" Dog is clearly confused by Mama's new Denny-inspired persona.

"And watch your language in my house!" she shouts.

Dog looks at me as if to say, *What is up with her?*

I shrug and look at the floor. "It's really okay if you don't feel up to having a stranger stay with us this weekend."

"Don't be silly. Go on and sign us up."

Hells bells!

Later on, Jackson calls while I'm stretched out on my bed. Mama brings me the phone. Luckily, Dog's been released from punishment, so he's out in the living room watching TV.

"You still mad?" Jackson asks me.

"Hurt," I say. "I wouldn't never cheat on you like that." And my nose starts in to stinging again.

"Come on, now. Don't think of it like 'at. Cain't you just be happy it made me realize I don't need nobody else?"

"Maybe," I say.

"It ain't like I called her up and asked her out."

"You *kissed* her."

"I kissed her *good-bye,* and thinking of you the whole time and how different it is when we kiss." His voice sounds all throaty. And suddenly I miss him so bad I can't hardly stand it.

"You promise never to do it again?" I sniffle.

"Yeah, I promise," he consoles.

"I guess I can forgive you then," I say, but I still feel bruised inside. I wanted us to be different, wanted us not to ever hurt each other, not to ever doubt.

"You glad to be home?" he asks.

"Always," I sigh, and tell him about the weekend plan, wishing I could just relax instead of having to deal with a houseguest.

"Don't *you* go falling for someone else now," he teases.

"Who, Jimmy?" I ask all shocked. "He's just a little shrimp. Besides, I couldn't do that to Stef . . . or you."

"I'm glad," he says. "I wish it was me coming for a visit."

"Me, too," I say, twisting up the blanket between my fingers.

"One of these days," he says.

"When?" I ask, knowing he'd ruther I didn't.

He don't say nothing. Then finally he goes, "I best run. Say hey to that Jimmy for me."

"Oh, hush," I reply.

Well, we did not get stuck with Jimmy the Great for the weekend, no, sir. He got placed with ol' Miss Caroline. Now poor Stef ain't got a chance in hell of slipping out for any hanky-panky. But I ain't got time to be too worried about her. I'm more concerned for myself. 'Cause you see, what we got stuck with instead is some crazy seventeen-year-old guy named Hal who says he wants to be a preacher. That boy's got his nose in his Bible all daggum day. And since it was supposedly my idea, Mama says I've got to spend time with him, join in on the group activities, and show him around. Stef is going to owe me big-time for this one. Personally, I believe Mama's just trying to get me out of her own hair so's she can woo old Denny Caterpillar. Yuck!

I've got to take Hal on down for the first church event. We ride bikes (he's on Dog's). This dude barely knows how to ride. His balance is all wiggly-woggly; he doesn't know about standing up to get up the hill; he doesn't even know how to jump the dang thing up over the curb. It's embarrassing.

Even though it's a short ride, I feel worn out by the time we get to the church. I'm about ready to tear into Stef. But she's tagging along behind Jimmy looking like a pathetic little puppy. Suddenly, I ain't got the heart. His face may be full of bumps, and he may have a two-dollar haircut, but when he takes hold of her hand, damn, I go green, wishing Jackson were here to take mine.

I try to hang back and just be an observer, using my inhaler treatments as an excuse, but the preacher pulls me in and makes me participate. It's one event after the next—icebreaker games and acting out Bible stories and fixing a community dinner. By the end of the day, I have had it. I can see how happy Stef is, so I try not to hold a grudge for getting me into this mess. But I can't help wondering how God chooses whose prayers to answer.

I'm glad I've got the excuse of nighttime to be left alone, except of course for Dog snoring in the next bed over. Him keeping me awake means I got all kinds of time to lay there and ponder what Jackson did. I just keep imagining him kissing this Mary Elizabeth with her stuck-up nose and bouncy hair. Granted I've got no idea what she looks like, but in my mind, she's just petite and perky and perfect. I toss in the bed, trying to find a position where she ain't square in the middle of my brain. Dog lets out an extra loud snore.

It takes me forever, but eventually I do drift off. Next thing I know, the day is lightening and I feel a body creaking onto the bedsprings behind me. I turn around and holy hell! That bastard Hal is climbing naked into my bed!

"Ahhhhhhh!" I holler my dang head off.

Dog jumps up. Mama runs in and flips on the lights. And there is pervy old Hal, naked as a plucked hen! And here I am still hollering.

Mama gasps, covering her mouth.

"What the hell's a matter with you?" Dog yells at him.

Hal tries to look all innocent (which is pretty hard to do when you're standing there in your birthday suit) and points at me like I had something to do with it!

Mama and I both gasp.

"You dare to imply—" I begin, but Mama holds up her hand.

"Pack up your things this minute. I'm calling the preacher. And for heaven's sakes, get some clothes on!"

Hal slinks out of the room.

"Did he do anything to you?" Mama asks.

I shake my head. "I just woke up to find him slipping into the bed behind me."

Mama sighs. "Y'all go on back to sleep. I'll handle this."

But ain't nobody going back to bed now. Dog goes to the closet and pulls out his baseball bat.

"That ain't gonn' be necessary," Mama warns.

"I know," says Dog, and goes out to the living room with the bat in hand.

"You okay?" Mama asks.

I nod, still feeling shook up.

"You can go on back to bed if you like, or if you'd ruther, come on out to the kitchen and soon as we get rid of that boy, I'll make you some hot cocoa."

I stay real close to Mama as we go out to call the preacher. It seems right sweet the way Dog's acting all protective.

I can tell from Mama's end of the conversation that Preacher Paul thinks I had something to do with the goings-on in my bed, which ticks me off to no end. Nonetheless, he comes to get Hal and takes him back to his own house. And my church obligations are over for now. Amen.

Mama, Dog, and I sit up drinking cocoa, and somehow something's changed between the three of us. We don't got to talk about it or nothing. But it's kind of like when me and Mama are at the hospital. It's Us against Them.

"I'd a taken that bat right to his head if you'd needed me to," Dog assures me.

"Thank you." I smile.

He cuts on the TV and we all watch cartoons on the couch, cuddled up under a blanket. We haven't done that since Dog and I were little.

But word spreads quicker through a church than chicken pox through a preschool, and before long the phone is ringing off the hook. I let Mama and Dog deal with it. Through one of them calls, we come to find out Stef tried to sneak into ol' Miss Caroline's to rendezvous with Jimmy. I can't even believe she'd be that bold. When Miss Caroline found them in a compromising position, Jimmy went and blamed it all on Stef, and now they ain't even talking! There's some strange irony right there. I'm just grateful this weekend is coming to its end.

When the phone rings again, I notice Mama's voice sounds different. It doesn't take long for me to figure who she's talking to.

Dog watches her awhile, then turns to me. "We in trouble, now, sis. I can just see it coming."

"Denny Caterpillar," I say, nodding my agreement.

And Dog answers, "Lord save us all."

22

Mama sure does act weird when old Denny comes around. I don't get it. 'Cause if she plans on staying together with him, doesn't she think he's going to come to find out what she's really like? How long can she keep up the fakey laughing and all that mess?

I go hide in my room and read through some printouts I made at the library about course choices for that program in the mountains. I know it's only dreaming. But I reckon if you go on and act like something is real, sometimes it just believes you. Next thing you know, there it is staring you in the face.

Stef calls on the phone, sounds like she's been crying.

"What's wrong?" I ask her.

"Jimmy broke up with me," she sobs.

"What all happened?" I ask.

"That night he was in town, we met back behind Miss Caroline's. I figured we'd be safe meeting outside. We were a ways past kissing when she came down, though she should rightly have been asleep by then. Jimmy said it was all my idea, like he had nothing to do with it, as if I dragged him out of bed and forced him outside. I was so mad! But then, after he left, I called him in Georgia and asked him why he did that. He ignored my question and said he didn't think we were right for each other."

"No!"

She sniffles. "Why would he say that?"

"Oh, Stef, you deserve better."

"But I wanted *him*," she sobs.

"I'm sorry, hon."

"I'll get over it. Enough about his sorry butt. What's going on with you?" she asks.

"You sure you're gonn' be okay?"

"Yeah. Just distract me. Tell me what all is happening in your life."

"Listen to what Joie said when I called her from the hospital," I say.

"What?" Stef asks halfheartedly.

I launch into a slightly dramatized version of the conversation.

"Some friend," Stef cries. "Can't trust anybody."

"V!" Denny calls from the kitchen. This is a new nickname he came up with for me, and he has stuck to it like white on rice.

"I better go," I say. "Feel better."

I come out there to find Mama and Denny all giggly and looking at me like they've got some big secret or something.

"What?" I ask, feeling edgy around their swooning.

They stare at each other, grinning like a couple of cats that ate the canaries.

"Are y'all planning on spilling the beans or what?" I ask.

Finally, Mama glances up at me from where she's sitting at the table, her feet up on a chair and she goes, "Denny, you go on and tell her. It's your surprise."

He's washing up their supper dishes (I ate in my room), and he says, "That's a'ight. It was your idea."

"And . . ." I encourage, hoping they'll get on with it.

"Don't you be sassy," Mama says. "We got a nice surprise for you. So just keep your shirt on."

I sigh and try my best not to roll my eyes, quite frankly afraid to hear what it is they expect me to be all fired up about.

"Denny's in real bad need of a painter this weekend, got a job and one man short," she says, looking at me all knowingly.

"So?" What in hell has this got to do with me? I know they don't expect me to be out there working in this heat.

"I'm surprised at you. Don't you see?" Mama asks, all excited. "It's the perfect chance for Jackson to come down for a visit."

My heart starts to beating real fast, but I know I ain't got a prayer. "Thank y'all for the thought," I sigh, "but his mama wouldn't never let it happen."

There they go, grinning at each other again. Denny dries his hands on a dishtowel and takes over the seat where Mama's feet were at. He starts to rub them for her.

"What?" I ask, sensing there's more to this story.

"Denny done called Jackson's mama already," she squeals.

"Are you for real?" I ask, afraid to get my hopes up. Mama nods all excited. "What did she say?"

"Well, now," Denny begins, "she was hell-bent on saying no when

I first brung it up—'scuse my language, darlin',' he adds to Mama.

Get on with it, I'm thinking, struggling to hold my tongue.

Denny continues, "I told her he had a reputation for being a reliable hard worker and that's just what I was needing real bad. I promised her he'd get a nice paycheck and that I'd keep an eye on him while he was down here."

"And she said yes to that?" I ask, disbelieving.

He shakes his head. "Not at first. Till then she was still stuck on that no." He chuckles. "I assured her it would just be for the weekend, that we'd have him home by Sundy night. And then I added the real kicker, gave her the good ol' Southern mama kinda guilt saying how I admired the way he'd been working so hard to help her out since his daddy passed."

My mouth is literally hanging open. "How did you . . . I mean, where did you . . . ?" I can't seem to find my words.

Denny chuckles, all proud of himself. "Course I told her I knew of him through you and that you'd filled me in on things."

Ho-ly cow! "He's coming?"

"This very weekend," Denny says.

"Oh—my—gosh! I mean, thank you, both of y'all. I can't even believe it! What time will he be here?"

"Slow down, girl," Denny laughs. "He don't even know yet hisself. His mama's fixing to tell him when he gets home from work this evening. He'll drive down Fridy afternoon. I told his mama he can stay with me if'n his kin don't want him."

"They made up already. So I'm sure it's fine. But thank you, thank you!"

Some kind of crazy rush of something goes roaring through my chest. I feel like I'm going to explode from excitement. Before I even know what I'm doing, I run over and give Mama and even ol' Denny a hug. Then I run to my room, slam the door shut, cover my face with a pillow, and scream just as loud as I can.

Time is ticking by as slow as a donkey in the plowing field. Jackson should be on his way into town this very minute. Me and him are meeting for dinner at Eddie's Diner at six o'clock, like a real date. I'm just sick with worry about whether things will be different between us because of Miss Petite Perky Perfection.

Mama extended my curfew till eleven thirty, long as I promised no hanky-panky. And then, even though Jackson's got to paint tomorrow, I can still hang out with him over at the site, maybe help him out some. Soon as he's done, we've got the rest of the day together. He'll have to do a second coat on Sunday and then head home. But he's coming for real, and I know I am just rambling on, but Lord am I excited. I believe I'm going to go change my clothes again; I can't seem to find the right thing to wear. That sundress I wore to the church picnic looks the best on me, but after what happened that night, I believe it may have some bad juju.

I done fixed my hair and makeup fifty-eleven times already. Don't nothing seem perfect. The entire contents of my half of the closet are strewn across my bed. Makeup and hair products are positively littering every inch of space in the bathroom. DC (Denny Caterpillar—I can make up nicknames, too) is sitting out in the TV room giggling at my histrionics.

"Savannah, can you at least try to act normal?" Dog shouts through the bathroom door. "I got to go! Clear out."

"In a minute," I call.

"Dog, what are you hollering about?" Mama asks.

"Chaps my butt the way she thinks she's the only one lives here. The world don't stop just 'cause her boyfriend is coming to town. I need to go."

Mama knocks on the door. "All right now, shug. Give it a rest."

I was done anyhow.

"You look right beautiful," Mama says as I open the door.

However I look, I know it's got to be better than the last time Jackson saw me, since that was out at the hospital in Wilmington.

Finally, five thirty rolls around and I head out to walk into town. I make sure to take my inhaler with me, not wanting nothing to screw up our evening.

"You ain't leaving already, is ya?" DC asks, looking at his watch.

"I don't want to mess up my hair riding my bike. So I'm gonn' walk," I explain.

"We'll give you a lift in my truck," he says. "Sit tight while I call the office a minute, then we'll go."

I can't say no to that. Walking out in this heat is the last thing I want. DC goes into the kitchen to talk on the phone.

"What are y'all doing tonight?" I ask Mama, trying to pass the time like a sane person.

"We're going over to the isle for a nice dinner," she says, blushing. I swear she reads my mind, 'cause then she goes, "Don't think that means y'all are allowed to hang out here without supervision. I'll be home by nine anyhow."

"You and DC are getting along real well, huh?" I say, trying to be nice.

"DC?" she asks.

"He can call me V, I can call him DC," I say.

"What's the C for?" she asks.

"I don't know." I shrug her off. "What were you saying about him?"

She turns to hide a smile. "He's just good people, Vannah. Wants to treat me all the time, help with the washing up, even at work he makes me feel like a queen. He does get awful short-tempered with his crews, but he never takes it out on me." She waves it away. "I guess I just ain't used to somebody wanting to treat me all special like that without wanting something in return."

I always forget. She don't have nobody taking care of her. She's all the time looking after us. Ain't nobody but Gina looking out for her, and Gina's hands are near about as full as Mama's.

"How long's he gonn' be on the phone?" I ask, getting impatient.

"You don't need to show up twenty minutes early," she says.

I just want to get there already. Course if Jackson's late I might just lose it. He could still be on his way from Greenville for all I know, Friday traffic and all.

After a couple more minutes pass, I can't stand it one more second. "DC," I whisper real loud, pointing to where a watch would be on my arm if I wore one.

He puts his hand over the phone. "DC?" he asks.

I ignore him and point to my arm again. He holds up his finger, promising me he's almost done. I'm pacing the room, ready to pull my hair out, when he finally says, "Okay, I'll see ya tomorra, bye now."

Finally.

"Job's all set," he says, like he's trying to remind me that it's 'cause of him Jackson's here.

"Thank you," I say. "I really appreciate it. Now can we go?" And I head out the door. We all mash into his truck, Mama in the middle between me and DC. Dog rides in the back. I reckon they're dropping him off at Dave's. DC drives with one hand on Mama's knee and she's got her arm all tucked under his. Something about seeing her be physical with him gives me the heebie-jeebies.

"Have fun!" DC calls as I hop out of the truck in front of Eddie's.

"Y'all be good!" Mama adds.

Dog puts his hand up to his forehead and groans, "Oh, Jackson, Jackson!" and cracks himself up.

I don't say a word. I just run on into Eddie's hoping to get our regular table. I step inside to see if it's free, and Lord have mercy, Jackson's sitting there right in his old usual spot, waiting on me. He looks up and smiles that smile I couldn't seem to capture in my drawings, sparkling eyes and all. And Lord, but I just melt clear to pieces.

23

I can't hardly move I'm so keyed up. It's been weeks since we've been together. It feels like life has turned to slow motion—like in one of them romantic pictures you see on Lifetime TV or what have you, when the couple is running across some field into each other's arms—except of course we're not running through the diner. He's just standing up by his chair and smiling, kind of like frozen right there. And I'm the same over by the door. Finally I notice folks staring and I make my way over to the table. I reach his side and he leans down to kiss me—powerful, warm, and sweet, like he's trying to tell me how sorry he is with his kiss.

"I don't know what I was thinkin'," he says. And I know it's his way of apologizing.

We sit down and our faces are glowing—I can feel mine is just as bright as his looks.

Lois comes over and pulls an ink pen out of her big, peroxided hair. "Okay, lovebirds, y'all know what you want?"

I'm sort of embarrassed, but not really. I like hearing her call us that. Course I haven't even glanced at the menu yet. I shrug a little and Jackson says, "I believe we gonn' need a few."

Lois raises up her drawn-on eyebrows, smacks her gum, and goes to clear off another table.

Finally I find my voice. "I missed you real bad, Jackson." And I love the tickle of his name on my tongue when he's sitting there across from me.

"Don't you think for one minute I didn't miss you just as bad," he says, his voice sounding all husky.

Lordy, I'm blushing. I want to just go on and bawl and nag him about why he won't move back out here. But I force myself to hold my tongue. Instead, I say, "I sure am glad you're here now."

"Me, too," he says. "Now let's get sump'n to eat."

I look at the menu, but I seem to have lost my appetite.

When Lois returns, I'm still at a loss. Jackson orders a cheeseburger, fries, and a Coke.

"I'll have the same," I say, unable to think. She walks off and we go right on staring. "How was your drive?" I ask, feeling awkward.

"Slow," he grins. "I wished I could fly."

Ain't he just the sweetest?

"Everything okay at home?" I ask, wondering if his mama gave him a hard time about this trip.

He looks all serious suddenly, and for a minute I'm afraid he's going to tell me more terrible news.

"I want you to understand sump'n." He pauses, squirming, looking all uncomfortable. "What I'm doin' up there, stickin' by my mama when she needs me, I'm doin' it in part for you."

I feel real bad that here he is opening up and I ain't got a clue as to what he's talking about.

"You understand?" he asks.

I shake my head no.

He shifts in his chair. "If I was to run out on her when she needs my help, what would that say to you about the kinda man I am? If I was to up and take off, who's to say I wouldn't do the same to you someday? I want you to know you can count on me, Savannah, that I ain't the leavin' type."

I can't hardly believe my ears. Imagine him, the strong, silent sort going to the trouble of saying all that! Shew! I don't know how to respond. I mean, I'm all choked up with feelings, nary a word coming out. I grab me a big bite of air and just launch into it. "That was the sweetest, most wonderful thing anybody has ever said to me in my whole entire life." And good googly moogly, but tears trickle right out of my eyes! I wipe them away real quick. "I hadn't thought about it like that. I kinda thought of it more like you were choosing her over me." And feeling ashamed, I look down in my lap, relieved that I didn't nag him earlier on.

He reaches over and tips my face up so we're looking each other square in the eye. "I couldn't never do that," he says. "And taking Mary Elizabeth out that night, I swear I wasn't two-timin' you. I was thinking about you every minute, about how nobody compares to you." His face is all serious, and his lower lip is near quivering.

Then Lois bustles over with our food and asks us all sorts of dumb questions about condoms, I mean *condiments*! Lord a'mighty!

Jackson starts to eating, but I can't quit staring at him. I drink my Coke, but I just ain't hungry. He gets embarrassed, being watched like that, and starts laughing. He pours some ketchup on my plate, salts it up, and feeds me a few fries dipped in it, just the way I like them. And I tell you, I don't give a rat's derrière who's watching.

Jackson pays for dinner and suggests heading out to the beach, and I can't think of any place I'd ruther be.

"Y'all come back now, y'hear," Lois calls as we head outside.

Jackson holds the door for me, then opens his truck for me, too— a real gentleman. We hop on in and ride out to the beach. He parks in the nearly empty lot, and we sit for a spell, staring out at the sky as it changes colors. I'm tucked up under his arm, leaning my head against him and wishing we could stay like this forever.

"You painted any pictures since you been home?" I ask him.

"One."

"Good for you. Did you bring it to show me?"

He turns to me with a peculiar look on his face. "I brung it for you to keep," he says.

"Are you for real?" I practically scream.

We go out to the back of the truck, and he pulls out a picture of the beach, an abandoned surfboard laying in the sand.

"I thought it might remind you of that day, y'know?" he says.

I hug him as tight as I can. "I love it," I squeak out when I find my voice. "It's amazing." The ocean looks like it's coming right at you, the sand like it'd be soft to the touch. And off the scene, I can just imagine us playing and kissing and all. I'm overtaken by the beauty of what hides inside of him.

A couple of folks walking by take a look over our shoulders and mumble about how good his picture is.

"We ought to bring it by and show it to that guy at the junior college," I say.

He shrugs and sets the painting back in the truck under a blanket. Then he takes my hand and we head down towards the ocean. Jackson stands behind me and puts his arms around me, warming me, melting away the gooseflesh that has crept up onto my arms. His body behind me feels like a big ol' blanket or some kind of safety net, one.

Staring out to the sea, I say, "You gonn' be a real painter someday, you know, like the kind what shows his work in a gallery and sells his pieces."

"I'on't know 'bout that," he says.

"It's what you want, though," I say, "ain't it?"

He's awful quiet. I turn to face him and ask him with my eyes.

"Life just ain't that simple, Savannah. Regular old folks like us don't just get to choose like 'at."

I ain't even angry at him for saying such nonsense, 'cause it's clear as day that it's just sadder'n hell that he feels that way, like he got old too quick. I tell him, "I'ma hold that dream for you. You mark my word. I ain't never gonn' let it slip away."

"Then I'll hold yours," he says. "College, right?"

I nod, smiling, and tick it off for him. "Gettin' the hell out of this hole, getting a job I can count on, traveling the world."

"Maybe we can travel together," he says.

He squeezes me real tight, then takes my face in his warm, rough hands, and kisses me like nobody's business. Before I know it, we're down in the sand and I can't think of nothing but getting closer to him, wanting to bring our two selves into one, like there's just a fire inside of me that's going to rage until we do. And I can feel how much he wants it, too.

But then he pulls away, breathing real hard. He sits up and puts his head in his hands, pulling on his hair.

"What's wrong?" I ask him.

"Nut'n," he says. "We just got to slow it down is all." Then he smiles at me real big and takes my hand. "Come on, let's go."

We walk along the beach, and I tell him all the details about Mama and DC and how they got together, how strange it was that the sign I felt sure was for him might just have been meant for her, except of course now he's here to paint for DC, so maybe it was for him after all, too. I tell him all about Stef and Jimmy and that crazy Hal. When I'd told him all this on the phone, it felt more like reporting on my day-to-day activities, but now, it's different, like we're connected, and somehow that helps me understand my own feelings better.

I ain't never been a big churchgoer. And I don't mean to be blasphemous or nothing, but right now in this moment, I find myself feeling like a devout member of the church of Love. I reckon Mama would say I'm just a hopeless romantic. Maybe them folks from Jane Eyre's Victorian era would think I'm immoral. But I swear, there ain't nothing else in the world this pure.

24

I didn't hardly sleep a wink last night, floating on a cherry cloud. I should probably wait awhile, give Jackson some time to get into his groove with the painting and all. But I don't think I can hold up even one more second. I know he's supposed to be at the building site at seven thirty. I believe I'll pack him up some biscuits and jam and a Thermos of coffee, just in case he didn't get a chance to eat at his cousins' beforehand. Lounging in bed just a moment longer, I stare at the painting he brought me, which is leaning up against the wall. His talent just leaps off the canvas.

I try to be real quiet in the kitchen. But sometimes things just bang when you don't intend for them to.

"Savannah, what in the world are you doing up so early? It ain't but seven o'clock," Mama whines, dragging herself out to the kitchen and helping herself to the pot of coffee I just brewed.

"I couldn't sleep no more. I figured on bringing Jackson a little something in case his kin weren't up yet to fix nothing for him."

"Lord, child. I reckon he can find breakfast all on his own." Mama shakes her head. Then she says, "If you're taking some up there, though, you may as well bring enough for Denny and the others, too."

And before I know it, she's packing up a great big basket of a feast, with cut melon and sausage and bacon and even fried eggs!

I start laughing. "Mama, there ain't no way this mess is gonn' be good by the time I done drug it up there."

Her face like to fall in on itself for a minute, then she smiles real big. "Okay," she says, "hop in the car. Give me a minute to fix my face and I'll run you up there."

I pack all that food up into the car and sit down to wait for her. I've got to admit she sure is changing for the better with DC in the picture. He may irritate me something awful at times, but he does seem to have a calming effect on Mama. Plus, now that he's gone and brought Jackson to me, he's pretty much bought my approval.

When we arrive, Jackson is already hard at work, painting like it's the most important job there is, all focused and serious. Dag, but he makes me proud. Them other guys ain't even started yet, just hanging about laughing and being silly. I can see he's made an impression on DC. Soon as we walk up, DC points to Jackson and raises his eyebrows up at Mama as if to say, *I knew we could count on him.*

I reckon Mama was right. DC sure does have his good points.

When Jackson sees me, his eyes light right on up, but then he looks sort of awkward, like he ain't exactly sure what to do. He looks over to DC for authorization or what-have-you. He is his boss after all.

"You eat yet?" DC asks him as Mama and I unload the picnic basket. "Smells mighty good."

Jackson shakes his head no.

"Come on over here and grab some of this grub yer lady brung us, 'fore the boys clean it out!" he yells.

I hate to see that beautiful picnic getting tore up like that by all them hands. Ain't exactly how I pictured the whole thing.

Jackson snags a biscuit and scoops some fried egg onto it. Then he walks over to me and gives me a quick kiss on the lips. "You do all this?" he asks. I smile. And I swear on the Holy Bible, but there is a wave of heat between us like to set a forest on fire. "Thanks. It's good." He finishes it off in two bites. "I reckon I best get back to work."

And I understand. I may not like it. But I get it.

"Come on, V," Mama says. "We can check back with the boys later on."

"I think I'll stay and watch awhile, if it's okay," I say. "I promise not to get in the way," I add, looking first at Jackson, who nods, then at DC, who shrugs.

After Mama goes, I find me a shady spot and literally watch Jackson paint, the way his arm moves up and down, the way he's careful around the edges, the way he wipes the sweat from his brow onto his shirtsleeve. I'd like to stay and watch him all day. But the smell of that paint is rightly teasing my lungs, triggering my dang asthma. Even with the daily meds, something this strong messes with me.

I take a few pulls on my inhaler and walk a ways from the building to get me some fresh air. And law, but one of my special feelings comes slamming over me like a big old tidal wave smashing me down to the ocean floor. The feeling is so big and so exciting, I can't hardly contain it, and I feel like I might pass right on out.

I reckon DC must have seen me swooning. He comes running over and holds me up. "Savannah! Y'okay? You need a go to the hospital?"

His stinky old smell of sweat and cigars brings me back down to earth. "Naw. I'm okay. Just had a little episode. It ain't nothing."

He sets me down in the shade and carries on about the fumes being bad for my breathing and maybe he ought to tote me on home. I just wave him off, not caring about nothing, 'cause the feeling I had, the big old walloping feeling that came over me, was the sense of me and Jackson being together again, that this just feels right. I reckon it could mean he'll be visiting real soon, maybe even regularly, who knows.

I go up behind him and whisper, "You're awful cute when you're paintin'."

He tries to hold back his grin. "Shut up, girl. You best go on home."

I can't help myself, though. "You tired of me already?" I ask, as I accidentally on purpose lean up against him for a moment.

He drops his paintbrush right in the dirt. "Savannah!" he whispers, looking embarrassed.

Ol' DC looks our way and yells, "V! You best get out his way if'n you want that boy to be done 'fore dark."

I smile real big at him, but inside I'm rolling my eyes something serious. "I guess I'll go on and get going then," I say to Jackson. But I wait to see if he protests.

"I'll come get you soon as I clean up," he promises, which sends a thrill right on up my chest.

I make as if I'm leaving, but I can't bring myself to do it. I find a spot behind some trees and watch him lose himself in the steady motion of color. Them other guys are using spray guns and rollers, but DC trusted all the detail work to Jackson, seeing as he's a real painter and all.

After a while, Jackson goes over to a bucket of turpentine to clean his brushes, and without any effort to find me, he looks directly at me and winks! I reckon he knew I was here all along. That wink only makes the heat inside me flare up even worse. I best head down to the beach for a swim before I'm accused of arson. I use DC's phone to call Mama, and she agrees to come give me a ride.

The day drags. Ain't nothing fun when I know Jackson is so durn close by and still so dang far. It's like my body knows he's near and it just won't settle down. I try the beach, the hammock, the TV, music. I even go to work at the library for a few hours, even though I'm not scheduled for today.

Back at home, I start cleaning up our room, but Dog's shoes are so stinky I can't hardly stand it.

Have you ever noticed how much you can tell about a person by their shoes? Seriously now, it's quite informative. Mama, she wears low heels—pretty, but practical. Both of the pairs she owns used to be colorful, but now they're all faded and worn.

Me, I wear flip-flops. I get a new pair from the Family Dollar Store at the beginning of every summer, and come fall they are clean wore through. This year they're blue with green polka dots. I reckon flip-flops say I go on and let everything out, which I believe is true about me—honest and forthcoming.

Jackson mostly goes barefoot when we head down to the beach, a sure sign that he's a trustworthy soul—nothing to hide. But when we go out, he wears his work boots all tied up tight, which explains why he has a hard time sharing his feelings.

Then there's Dog, whose feet are so offensive, seems like any pair of shoes he puts on just curls up and dies. He's got about fifty-eleven pair of tennis shoes, most of them outgrown—all just as smelly and worn as a cowboy's old boot. You know what them cowboys are always stepping in. Yep, and Dog is sure full of it.

Forget cleaning this pigsty.

I go out to the kitchen to call Stef, thinking maybe she'd like to meet Jackson later on.

"Hey, what's up?" I say.

"Nothing." She sounds gloomy.

"Why so glum?" I ask.

"I miss Jimmy, and I hate him, too."

"Don't cry," I say as she starts in to whimpering. "I'm sorry he blamed you at Miss Caroline's. And may I just say he's an idiot for dumping you."

"You're lucky Jackson ain't like that."

"You want to come out with us this evening? I'm sure he won't mind. You haven't even met him yet."

"That's okay. I'd just be a third wheel."

"Come on now. You're my best friend."

"Y'all don't hardly get to spend any time together. He won't want me hanging around."

"I want you. You've just got to meet him."

"Some other time, Van. I've got big plans to lay on the couch and watch sappy movies and cry all night."

"That sounds real productive."

"I'll talk to you later on," she says.

After we get off the phone, I find my current romance—*Love, Lace, and Lemon Cakes*—under the coffee table and snuggle up on the couch. 'Fore I know it, I'm all caught up in the story and next thing I realize, it's time to get ready.

By five o'clock I'm showered and dressed and waiting by the window. The clock in the kitchen is ticking louder than a rat pack in a pantry. My book was at an exciting part, so I pick it up again. Just when the big brute and the helpless young woman are fixing to, well, consummate things, I hear a truck pulling into the gravel driveway. I drop the book and jump up. But it's only DC coming to fetch Mama for dinner.

The clock says 6:15. Maybe DC will at least be able to tell me what's going on. "Are y'all just finishing?" I demand soon as he steps foot in the door.

"Hello to you, too," he says.

"Hey. But seriously, now, where is he at? Why'd y'all have to work so late?"

He gives me a long, hard look, then busts out laughing. "Lordy, V, you got it bad, huh girl?" He shakes his head. "Don't you worry your purty little head none. They's predictin' some weather tonight, so's we had to get things covered up. Your boy cut out 'bout thirty minutes back. I reckon he'll be here 'fore long."

And no sooner does he finish yapping than another truck pulls up—a blue one, the only one that matters. "Bye!" I call, heading for the door.

Mama comes rushing out of her room. "Y'all behave yourselves! And be back by curfew!"

I hear DC whispering something at her and she adds, "Oh, all right, you can stay out till eleven thirty, but no messing around, y'hear?"

"Yes, ma'am!" I call. *Thank you,* I mouth to DC. He winks at me. Then I run out the door before she can change her mind.

Jackson's standing there all sparkly clean, his hair still wet from the shower. He licks his lips, looking nervous as all hell.

"Hey," I giggle. Guess I'm sort of nervous, too.

"You look right beautiful." He smiles, reaching for my hand.

I glance down at his shoes real quick—yep, work boots. I'm going to have to do something about that.

I want to kiss him real bad, but I look back and, sure enough, there's Mama staring out at us from the window. So I grab his hand and we get up into the truck.

"Hungry?" he asks.

"Not really," I say. Food seems so inconsequential.

"Me either. Mind going for a ride?" he asks.

Imagine that—a boy that ain't hungry. I scoot closer to him. He cuts on the radio. It all feels too perfect, except for he hasn't said much, and I sure wish he would. I don't know what to ask to get him started talking.

"How was your day?" I finally begin, thinking that sounds like a naggy old housewife.

"A'ight." He shrugs.

"How was paintin'?" I prod.

He nods, then looks at me and smiles. "Good."

Lord, how do I get this boy to speak in more than one-word sentences? "I liked watching you," I say. "You looked . . . real focused, you know? Like I could tell you was really into it and all."

He don't say nothing.

"Why so quiet?" I ask.

He shrugs. "It's just too good, too right." We sit quiet awhile. "I liked the work today. I mean, it ain't exactly the same as paintin' pitures. But you cain't make no money doin' that. It's closer to it, though, and a whole helluva lot better than that old machine shop. Left me feeling quiet is all."

He pulls into a parking area looking out over a deserted stretch of beach I've never been to before. It ain't dark yet, plus if Mama's easing up on curfew, maybe we can bend the other rules a bit as well. She didn't actually say anything about them still being in effect. He grabs a blanket out of the back of the truck and we walk down to the sand.

Not one second after we lay down, we start making out. I can't hardly help myself and neither can he. And it feels so good to have his hot mouth on mine, to feel his tongue, so gentle and warm. . . . Not like this one guy I kissed last year—Cory Hallman—who stuck his tongue practically down my throat.

As much as I'm loving every minute of this, I can't help but wonder, with nobody around, no threat of somebody telling Mama, what's to stop us from going all the way? And am I ready for that? And what about protection? Whoo, I done scared myself silly. I pull away.

"What's wrong?" he asks, looking worried.

"Nothing," I say, only that ain't the entire truth, but then, I ain't at all sure what is.

"S'okay," he says, all tender, "we can slow down." And he pulls me real close and just stares into my eyes like he's seeing God.

"You ever gone all the way?" I ask him. He don't say nothing. "Yeah, you have. I can tell." I wonder if it was with Mary Elizabeth, but I don't ask.

"You haven't," he says, like it's all right.

I shake my head.

He shrugs. "It don't matter none. We won't do nothing you ain't ready for, okay?"

I feel so happy inside—not just 'cause he doesn't mind waiting, but 'cause I know in my gut I've got me one of the good ones.

The air is damp and warm tonight, my breathing just as clear as day. I ain't never felt better.

"Okay if we kiss some more?" he asks.

I don't need words to answer that one.

It starts to drizzle on us. We just laugh and snuggle up closer. But the sky has a strange greenish look to it, and then the wind picks up and the sand starts to blowing all around. We haul ourselves up and back into the truck.

"Look like a storm coming," Jackson says, watching the clouds.

And then, real sudden-like, the sky seems to open right on up and big, fat drops are smacking against the windshield. It's coming down so hard we can't see nothing but rain. The wind is crazy loud, and I admit I'm getting scared.

Jackson cuts on the radio and searches for a news station. The man says there's a tornado hitting the northeast side of Morehead, which, of course, is just exactly where we're at. Scared as I am, I can't help being grateful that the tornado I was named after wasn't heading in this direction fifteen years ago. What kind of life would I have had with a name like Morehead?

There ain't no way to drive in this mess. So we just cuddle up close to each other and wrap ourselves in the damp blanket.

Lightning crackles across the sky—just two seconds till the thunder hits—meaning it ain't but two miles off! Hail starts smacking the windows and bouncing up. It's getting awful creepy.

And then, Lord have mercy! In the next bolt of lightning, Jackson points just a hair northward and we can actually see the twister! And the wind is blowing something fierce. The man on the radio is warning everybody to take cover, to get out of mobile homes and cars. But where else are we going to go?

Jackson takes my hand. "Savannah, you trust me?" I nod. "We gonn' have to get out the truck."

"Are you crazy?" I ask, looking out at the wildness of the storm.

"It ain't safe here. That twister could head our way any second. It'll pick this truck up like it's a Tonka."

"It'll pick *us* up just as easy!" I shout over the din of the wind.

"Not if we stay low. Come on."

And then we see in the flash of lightning, that cyclone is heading towards us.

Jackson grabs my hand and pulls me out into the maelstrom. We run against the lashing rain till we find a ditch, then lay down in it. He covers my body with his own.

"I'm scared," I call out, my body shivering despite his heat.

"Shh," he says. "It'll pass. We'll be fine." And then he starts talking, yelling over the noise, I imagine to calm me down. "My daddy used to call twisters the devil's tail. We'd wait 'em out in the cellar when they'd come through, and he'd tell us stories about storms he'd seen when he was comin' up."

"I was named after a tornada that was heading for Savannah, Georgia!" I shout, laughing at the absurdity of the whole situation.

Lightning cracks open the sky, with thunder right on its heels. I grab on to Jackson real tight. Just then, we hear a crash, but the devil's tail swirls on out to the ocean, taking the wind and driving rain along with it.

We wait awhile, laying side by side in the ditch. I'm real glad for his warmth and calm beside me.

He wipes the wet hair out of my face and smiles. "Named after a tornada, huh? Life with you sure ain't dull."

We laugh and look into each other's eyes.

"Savannah," he says, sounding all serious.

I touch his lips with my fingers, almost wanting to shush him, afraid of what might come out.

"I love you," he says with this look in his eye like he almost can't bear it.

"Hallelujah!" I cry, making him laugh again. "I love you, too." And he kisses me real good.

As the rain lightens to a drizzle and the wind chases the twister out to sea, we head back to the truck. It's just where we left it; the cyclone didn't get it. But the windows are all smashed. We climb in, soaking wet, and clear the glass off the seat with the blanket.

Suddenly I realize I am starved. I wish we could go out to dinner like we had planned on. But I know we got no choice but to head home—what with the truck a mess and us soaking wet and all.

Mama's going to be fit to be tied.

25

Mama and DC are already home when we get there. Apparently, they gave up on eating out, concerned about where we were all at during the storm. Mama nearly flips when she sees us, wet and bedraggled.

"Come in the house this minute!" she yells. "Good Lord, Savannah, y'all could have been killed."

"We're okay," I tell her. "Jackson knew what to do."

She glares at him and scolds, "Y'all should have come straight home once you heard about the storm."

"Sorry, ma'am, but by the time we heard about it, we needed to head for cover."

"Don't fret now, Porsha," DC says. "They did a'ight."

"Get dried up and I'll fix us some supper. Gina should be here any minute with Dog. I'm guessing you didn't eat yet."

"No, ma'am," Jackson replies.

DC brings Jackson a clean sweatshirt and pair of jeans he had in his truck. They don't fit too well, but at least they're dry.

Then Dog tramples into the house. Gina honks out front and Mama and DC run out there to check in with her.

"Did y'all see that twister?" Dog asks, his eyes glowing with excitement. "That was the coolest thing ever. We heard it picked up two cows over at the Larsons' farm and set 'em back down by the Kellys'. Damn, Savannah, you look like hell. What happened to you?"

"Me and Jackson got caught in the storm."

"Where were you at?"

"The beach up by Morehead," I say.

His expression changes and his tone turns obnoxious. "Up at the beach at night, huh?"

"Hush," I warn.

"Don't worry. I won't tell Mama," he says, just as she and DC walk back in.

"Won't tell Mama what?" she asks, sounding concerned.

"Nothing," I say, giving Dog the stink eye. Seeing this as a good moment to exit, I go get cleaned up. Then we all eat Mama's fried chicken and corn on the cob. After dinner, we all five of us watch a movie together. I even get to snuggle up with Jackson on the couch without Mama saying a word against it.

When the movie ends, Mama and I wash up the dinner dishes. Jackson wanders over and puts his chin in his hand on the counter, just staring at me.

"Quit!" I tell him. He's embarrassing me.

"What?" he asks.

"Find something else to look at," I say, even though I am, of course, loving every minute.

He starts flipping through a *People* magazine that's laying on the counter. After a few more minutes, he goes, "What's this?" holding up a letter addressed to me from school.

"I don't know," I say. "Probably just my schedule for the fall." But this little bitty piece of me is wondering—what if it might could be about that program in the mountains?

"Did I forget to show you that?" Mama asks. "I believe it arrived a week or two ago. I'm sorry. I thought I told you about it."

Jackson gets a mischievous smile on his face and opens the letter. "Let's see what courses Savannah's gonn' be taking this year." He opens the envelope and I race over to grab it away, scared that if it is my schedule, looking at it'll make it happen—just like with ol' Miss Caroline's whiskers. He runs through the living room and I chase after him, tackling him to the floor in front of the TV. We're laughing. Mama and DC are smiling, watching us.

"Move!" Dog shouts. "I can't see."

Jackson slides to the side and looks at the letter. "This ain't no schedule," he says.

A strange feeling of dread rolls right over me. I grab the letter from him.

Dear Savannah Brown,

You have been selected for the honor of spending the upcoming semester in the Program for Promising High School Students at the University of North Carolina at the Asheville campus in the beautiful Blue Ridge Mountains. This program is designed for the best and the brightest and will be attended by students from throughout the Carolinas. Attendance in this program will strongly increase your chances for an academic scholarship to any one of the UNC campuses for college.

Please sign and return the enclosed acceptance form from the dean of the university no later than August 10th. Plan to depart for Asheville on the 30th. The program fee is $2,000 for the semester.

Congratulations! We are very proud of you and know you will represent our school with dignity.

Sincerely,
Principal Mary McTierney

There's a strange feeling in the pit of my stomach. I got it—the invitation to that program up in the mountains!

Jackson finishes reading over my shoulder. "Hell, girl! You didn't tell me you were *that* smart. But you best go on and send it in. It's nearly due."

"Send what in?" Mama asks.

While I sit there dumb, Jackson takes the letter out of my hand and brings it over to Mama. I'm nervous about her seeing the amount at the end.

She reads it through and covers her mouth with her hand. "Well, I'll be. Savannah, that is unbelievable! I am real proud of you, sugar. I don't know, though, Asheville sure is a long way off. What about your medical care? I'll call Dr. Tamblin tomorrow and see what he thinks."

"What's in Asheville?" Dog asks. "What the hell is everybody talking about?"

Mama shows the letter to DC on the couch and Dog reads over his shoulder.

"Some kind of goober fest that's gonn' be," Dog mutters, turning back to the TV.

"Savannah," Mama says, sounding all choked up. "How in the world did this happen?"

"Mrs. Avery put my name in for it. I didn't say anything 'cause it seemed so unlikely I'd get picked and all."

Mama shakes her head. "You did it, hon. You've been wanting to get outta this town since you could talk. You earned your chance. And a possibility of a scholarship to college!"

She's right, about all of it. So why is my stomach all tied up in knots? "What about Jackson?" I say, remembering that feeling I got just this morning that he'll be back again. "We been trying to find a way to be together all summer and his mama ain't likely to let him go gallivanting off to Asheville. I . . . I'm not sure about this."

Mama looks to Jackson for assistance.

"Savannah," he starts, real quiet.

"I got to think," I say. "Don't rush me." I feel like that ol' devil's tail has moved right into my gut.

Sunday morning DC called one of his contacts that knows a glass man who's going to come over and fix the windows on the truck.

I feel bad about not bringing breakfast up to the site today. But I am worn out, and I have a lot on my mind.

I've been thinking on how Jackson said he loved me last night. I reckon that storm brought us something good. Going through an experience like that binds people together somehow in a way I don't quite understand.

So when I consider that program—something I was hoping against hope I might get a chance to go to—I feel uncertain. And even if I did decide to go, how in the world would we afford it? Seems like there's no point even getting worked up over it.

Meanwhile, I can't stand that Jackson's leaving tonight. It doesn't seem right. I keep reminding myself about that feeling I had yesterday, about him being here again, about us being together. My feelings haven't never let me down yet—not even that yellow sign. He ended up working for DC after all. So he must be coming back, which means I simply just can't leave.

DC kept Jackson at the site till three. Now we've got barely a couple hours together before he has to drive back home. Having had our fill of nature for the time being, we head to the mall instead. We're walking around, holding hands, but it's like we ain't even on the same planet.

"You should go on that program. You know that, right?" he says.

I shrug, wondering for a moment how much I could save if I set aside every penny I make at the library the rest of the summer. "You hungry?" I ask him, seeing as he just about always is.

"I could eat," he says, not really seeming to care one way or the other. "You want some Chick-fil-A?"

What I want is to get out of this crowded place with all this stuff and lights and people and be somewhere where we can be together for real. I shake my head. "Let's go to Eddie's."

He's quiet all the way in the truck. It's driving me crazy. "Jackson, we ain't got but a little more time together. Why you so quiet?" I hate to nag, but I can't stand wasting our last itty bit of time like this.

"Sorry," he says. "I ain't too keen on leavin' or good-byes neither."

Which of course I'm glad to hear, but still. "Let's just try and don't think about it. Let's pretend like we got all the time in the world."

"I'm too old for pretendin'," he says.

We sit at our usual table at Eddie's. "What you gonn' get?" I ask him.

"I'on't know," he says.

Now that's unusual, him not knowing what to eat. I wasn't going to tell him about that feeling I had yesterday, 'cause he didn't react too good to the one about the yellow sign. But I've got to do something to cheer him up. "I got one of them special feelings," I say.

"'Nother train headed my way?" he teases halfheartedly.

I shake my head. Now, suddenly, I'm afraid to say it, afraid to jinx it, afraid it won't be real. "It's a secret," I tell him. "But, it's a good one."

"You just gonn' leave me hangin'?" he asks, all shocked.

I smile all flirty-like. And a certain look comes over his face like he finally figured out what he's hungry for.

We get up without ordering and head down to the beach—about the only place we can cuddle up and kiss. But it's busy as hell down there. We sure ain't going to get any privacy. We tuck ourselves down behind a dune and start kissing. But somehow it doesn't feel right. Instead of the soft, gentle Jackson of last night, he's more like an angry, frustrated Jackson. I try to slow him down. But he seems to be in his own little world.

"What is wrong?" I finally ask.

"Whatcha mean?" he replies.

"You seem different," I say.

He hangs his head. "I prob'ly should go. Mama wants me off the highway 'fore dark."

Forget about your mama! I want to yell. But I know he can't do that. And I know deep down in my heart, I don't want him to be the kind of guy that would. There ain't nothing right to say, so I just take his hand in mine and squeeze it real tight.

He looks at me all full of angst and pulls me to him, kissing me real hard like he's trying to take me into himself somehow, take some part of me along with him. I feel like I'm going to cry from wanting him not to go. But I know that won't help anything none. We hug each other real tight, not caring who's watching. Then we walk back out to the truck and he drives me home.

"Want to come in for a little while? Get something to drink 'fore you go?" I ask him.

He just shakes his head.

I can't do it. I can't get down out of the truck. 'Cause soon as I do, he's going to drive off and I'm going to die right here on the spot.

"Go on," he whispers.

I don't move.

"I love you," I say, as tears creep out my eyes, even though I'm trying my darndest to hold them back.

Looking like he might just cry himself if he opens his mouth to speak, he puts his hand behind my head and pulls me towards him and we kiss. And then I slip out of the truck without looking back at him, the only way I can. And he drives off without so much as a wave.

26

"Vannah! Get your butt off your shoulders and go breathe some fresh air!" Mama calls. She marches into my room, cuts on the lights and draws open the blinds. I hide my head under the covers.

"Looky here," she starts in. "I know you're all tore up about him leaving. I get it, I do. But you've got other concerns right now. You only have a handful of days left to send in that acceptance letter. Now get your butt up and get busy."

"Mama," I say. "I don't think I want to go to the mountains after all. It's too far. And I won't know anybody and—"

"I know you don't think I'm that dumb. Hon, you can't just give up on something you've always wanted because you might miss a visit from Jackson. Now I spoke to Dr. Tamblin and he thought it would be a real good idea you goin' up there."

"We can't even afford it," I blurt out.

"You let *me* worry on that one. You got to take advantage of the freedom you have to choose this, shug."

"I don't got any freedom at all," I say. "You get to have your boyfriend over any time you like, work whatever hours is convenient, even then get to hang out with him. I don't got a single choice about spending time with Jackson. It's up to everybody else when I get to see him. And Lord knows when that's gonn' be!" I don't even know why I flip out like that, except I'm all confused about what to do about the program, and I don't like Mama making it seem like it's clear cut.

"Is that what you think? You got it so bad? I got all the freedom? Good God, Savannah! Who you think's been paying the bills every day of your life? Who's been through umpteen jobs? Who's the one worrying about you and your breathing and your safety and your brother, too? Not having a lick of energy left at the end of the day to go out and have a life of my own? Freedom? I hadn't had any of that since the day you were born. Now get your ass up out the bed and sign that letter!" And she storms right out of the room.

I feel like s-h-i-t. I ain't even sure what all is going on inside of me. The devil's tail is back, twisting up my guts. Am I mad? Hurt? Sad? I reckon some of all three. Mama ain't never talked to me like that, never made me feel like a burden, like she regretted having me. Let me tell you, that is one bad feeling, hearing somebody wish you weren't never born, specially when it's your own mother wishing it.

Okay, maybe I was being overly dramatic, maybe I overstated things a bit. But what she said, that was just uncalled for. I wish I could talk it through with Jackson. But I know he's at work, and he ain't allowed to take personal calls there.

I get dressed real quick and run outside to avoid crossing paths with Mama. I hop on my bike and ride out, touring the places me and Jackson went while he was here. I start at Eddie's and buy myself some hotcakes so I can sit at our table and recall every minute we spent there. Sadly, I ain't a bit hungry, so I just poke at them flapjacks and try to keep from crying. I go by the building site and the mall and down to the beach. I'd like to ride up to where we waited out the tornado, but I don't think my lungs are up for that sort of ride today. I ain't been breathing too right since the minute he left.

I lay down in the sand behind the dune where we kissed on Sunday and close my eyes. After a while, a shadow crosses in front of me.

"I been out looking for you everywhere," Mama says.

I don't open my eyes or show any sign I'm listening. But I feel all closed up tight inside, afraid to hear what's coming.

"I'm real sorry for what I said," she starts. "You sure made me mad, but I didn't mean none of that. You and Dog are the only things that matter to me in this whole world." She sits down beside me. "I like Denny a whole lot—I may even be starting to love him. But he ain't nothing compared to y'all. And I don't give a rat's ass about losing them jobs, don't blame you for your asthma. I was just p.o.'d by your attitude is all."

I sense her stretching out in the sand.

"Lord, I hadn't been out to lay in the sun in eons. Sometimes I forget we live by the beach a-tall."

"I thought you came to live down here 'cause you hated being away from the ocean," I say, letting the rest of it all slide by.

"It's true," she says. "I couldn't stand being landlocked. And even though I don't spend much time out here, it's like I got an umbilical cord stretching from me to the ocean and every time I get too far, it just don't feel right."

I reckon it's the reference to the umbilical cord that puts me in the mind of wondering about my grandma, 'cause next thing I know I'm asking her, "How come you don't talk to your mama? Why won't you tell us about her?"

Mama heaves a real big sigh. "Things had been bad between me and Mama for years. I suppose I held our poverty against her. We were poor as dirt when I was coming up. And I just couldn't rightly stand how she seemed to soak up all the pity the church folk gave us, bringing by used toys at the holidays and bags of groceries for Christmas dinner. I hated those donations, hated the uppity girls from school what delivered 'em. Guess I was ashamed."

She sits quiet, thinking, I reckon. I wait her out, hoping she'll say more. "She had a bum leg, my ma." She squints up at the sun, looking like it hurts her just to think about it. "She had polio as a child, and one leg never quite recovered. She used it, though, that handicap, used it to milk the church folk for pity, to get 'em to help her out and all. I hated the way she did that."

I can't hardly believe she never told me one lick of this before now. I ain't about to do anything that might cause her to stop talking.

"My mama hated your daddy something fierce," she goes on. "I reckon she knew he'd run off on me someday. I couldn't forgive her for that. I brought him home from Cary to meet her one summer, and she tried to stop me seeing him. She actually went and forbid me to go out with him a-tall. You can bet we cleared out of there pretty quick. When I was twenty, we ran off and eloped. I didn't talk to her again till after your daddy left us."

"What happened then?" I ask, too impatient to wait.

"She tore into me, telling me how she knew he was a no-count good-for-nothing piece of work, that she wadn't the least little bit surprised that he cut out. Then she told me I ought rightly move back home and raise y'all by her in her stinky old run-down double-wide trailer. And then she said the worst thing she coulda said to me. She said, 'Least we can count on the church to always be here for us.'" Mama shudders for real. "I got a piture in my mind of you and Dog getting them crappy hand-me-down gifts, me having to thank those same folks whose faces, full of pity, I'd been forced to thank for their broken games all those years and I said, 'Hell no! He-e-e-e-e-e-e-ll no!' I slammed that phone down and promised myself we wouldn't never take a handout or let nobody drown us in their pity ever again, not so long as there's air in my lungs. And I hope to God I've kept my word."

Lordy. I ain't never heard Mama go on like that. To think she never told us how she grew up, never shared one thing about what her mama was like. No wonder she didn't want to have the church folk come out to help us build on a room for Dog. And that's why she wouldn't tell her bosses about my asthma, why she'd ruther go on and lose the jobs than risk their pity.

I give her my biggest hug. "I'm sorry for everything I said, for every time I made you worry." I feel like I'm about to bust out in tears.

But she pulls me back and says, "Don't be sorry. And don't feel like you're some kind of burden. You are the light of my life."

And then she starts in to bawling! Can you imagine?

She wipes her eyes and says, "You did inherit one thing from my mama, though—thankfully just the one."

"What's that?" I ask, afraid to hear what she might say.

"Them special feelings you get sometimes, when you just seem to know what's coming? Your grandma got 'em too."

"She did?" I ask, all surprised. I can't even believe she never told me this.

"Spells, she called 'em. 'Havin' one of my spells,' she'd say. And then she'd go on about the feeling she had that this or that was fixing to happen. And sure enough, they were too true. Used to get her all worked up, like she was scared it was the devil's work or some such nonsense. I never understood why she couldn't just take them for the gift they were.

"When you were a little bitty thing and telling me what you sensed coming, I tried my best to make it seem like no big deal, hoping you'd learn to trust it as your very own guide, no fancy hocus-pocus, just a part of nature."

I had no idea. I never even thought about my special feelings being a gift or what-have-you or about Mama putting any effort into making me see them one way or another.

She hugs me real tight. "I may not have the gift of sight like you and your grandma, but I can tell you this, shug, everything's gonn' be all right."

I slump into her arms and just let myself believe it.

27

In the evening I sit on my bed, staring at the beautiful painting Jackson gave me that's hanging on my wall (covering up a few of those marks I made throwing my hairbrush), and call him, anxious to tell him all about what Mama told me at the beach. He sounds kind of down.

"Something wrong?" I ask him.

"Naw," he says. "You take care of that letter yet?"

"Not yet," I say. Then I change the subject by telling him what all Mama said about my grandma. I go on and on. "Can you imagine?" I say to end my little monologue.

"Hm," is all he says!

"Jackson, what is wrong with you, boy? I been waiting all day to tell you this and all you got to say is 'hm'?"

"I got some stuff goin' on I'm tryin' to figure out, is all."

"What stuff?" I beg. "Share it with me. That's what I'm here for."

He's real quiet. Then he goes, "I ain't exactly ready to talk about it yet."

Now it's all turning sour. "Do you not trust me to share your secrets with?" I say.

"Don't be like 'at," he says. "That ain't what I mean."

"Well, what do you mean, Jackson? Huh? Maybe you mean I'm too young to understand, or too naïve, or too dumb. Which is it?"

I hate when he goes all silent.

Finally he says, sounding put out, "I believe we best go on and hang up 'fore we say sump'n we gonn' regret. Talk to you soon." And then he clicks off! Damn!

I've got half a mind to call him right back, but I believe I'm going to let him stew in his own juices awhile. See how he likes that. Course none of this is helping my breathing none, which seems to have moved to a permanent state of raggediness. Mama's got me a doctor's appointment set up with my regular doctor, Dr. Tamblin, but it ain't for a couple more weeks. By then the summer will be near about fixing to end. I sure don't want to think about that.

I roam on out to the kitchen and pick at the tuna salad Mama's fixing for supper.

"It is just too hot out for cooked food," she says. "We gonn' have to make do with tuna salad sandwiches, pickles, chips, and some ice-cool lemonade—just like when we used to go on picnics when y'all were little."

I don't say nothing. I ain't feeling too chipper.

"That acceptance letter is near about due," she says.

"I know."

"What's wrong now, sad sack?" she teases.

"I just don't get why Jackson won't share his feelings with me. I tell him everything!"

Mama starts laughing.

"I'm glad you find my pain so funny."

"Now, now," she consoles. "You got to realize that guys are different than us. Lord, can you imagine Dog telling his feelings to some girl?" She shakes her head. "If they can't work everything out on their own, they just don't feel like men."

"You mean DC don't talk to you about things?"

"Some things," she says, mixing up the creamy tuna salad and spreading it onto the white bread. "Mostly, though, it's after he's got it all figured out. You set your expectations too high. It's not realistic, hon." She laughs. "You're hopeless."

Hope*ful*, I think. What's wrong with that? I wander back to my room, thoroughly dissatisfied by the conversation. Maybe I've been reading too many romance novels this summer. Or maybe I'm the crazy lady in the attic tying Jackson down, not his Jane Eyre at all.

I feel all raw and oozy like a rotten sore.

Pulling the damn acceptance letter off my dresser, I stare it down. I look at the curlicues of Mama's signature and at the blank line just above that. Then I jab my pen on the page, signing my name, sniffling away my tears. But then I dump the whole thing on the floor and crawl under the covers.

At supper I just pick at my food and try to keep my raggedy breathing under wraps so Mama doesn't go off the deep end. I sit and watch her and DC flirting. He eats with us nearly every night now.

"Y'all make me sick," Dog snaps. "Savannah, how can you stand to be around them? I'ma go stay over at Dave's. Between all this moping on one side and kissy kissy on the other, it's enough to choke a horse."

"Son," DC says, "don't be rude to your mama, now. I can't have that."

Dog looks at me and rolls his eyes.

"I suggest you apoleegize to her," DC insists.

"Denny, come on now, just let it go," Mama urges. "He didn't mean no disrespect." But she gives Dog that look that says, *You best behave.*

He's squirming under the pressure, not wanting to lose face. He looks just at Mama and mumbles, "I didn't mean nothing by it." Then he gets up and clears his plate.

"Course you didn't. He was just teasing," Mama says.

DC grunts.

"I'll phone Gina and tell her you're on your way," Mama calls after Dog.

"You don't got to do that," he snaps, turning back. "Don't treat me like a baby. Why can't you—"

"Fine," Mama interrupts, sounding stiff and seriously p.o.'d to be talked to like that in front of her guest. "You go on. We'll talk about this tomorra."

"So you ain't gonn' call her, right? 'Cause that's just embarrassing, having your mama call like that when you're twelve years old."

"All right, go on then, Mr. All-Grown-Up."

Dog takes off and Mama winks at me. "I'll try and remember to call her later on about something else. You want to watch a movie with us?"

I shake my head and go hide in my room, not wanting to have to listen to her and DC giggling and being dopey the rest of the evening. I don't think Jackson and me act that dumb around each other. Missing him, I pick up that acceptance letter and hold it in my hands like I'm fixing to tear it in two. But then I just shove it back on my dresser and pull out my journal instead.

I don't sleep too good. Between my breathing and my bad dreams, I just wish the dang night would go on and end. As I get up about seven o'clock, I promise myself I will not call Jackson Channing again till he calls me first.

It's story time at the library again. Only today it's a bunch of rowdy preschoolers. The moms hang out at the back of the room chatting, while I try to keep their kids sitting on their butts and listening to the book. They're bouncing around and making noise, giving me a headache. I fear I may soon find myself with another shoe fight on my hands, so I scrap the standard choices in the story time basket and pull one of Dog's old favorites off the shelf, *What! Cried Granny.* The kids finally quiet down and even join in, just yelling on the refrain. By the end, they're all laughing, and of course, every one of them wants to check it out for the week.

As they scatter, Miss Patsy comes over and puts her hand on my shoulder. "Nice job there," she says. "You really held their attention."

"Dog always liked that one when he was little," I say.

"Your mama told me about that program you were invited to at UNC-Asheville. I'm real proud of you."

"Thanks," I say, knowing that my time is nearly up to decide what I'm going to do about that durn thing. The deadline is nearing and I still haven't sent it in. I wanted that invitation so bad earlier on. Why can't I figure out what I want now?

On Thursday morning, I take Jackson's painting off the wall and walk all the way over to the junior college. It's killing me that he hasn't called. I reckon I'm secretly hoping this will give me a reason to phone him. When I poke my head into the art gallery, I'm disappointed to find a young woman at the desk.

"Can I help you?" she says.

"I was looking for someone else," I reply.

Just then, the man I met before with the wild gray hair pokes his head out of a back room. "Well now," he says. "I remember you. I had a notion it was your own work you were speaking of."

Smiling, I say, "No, sir. I'm not this talented. My friend is just shy about showing off his work, so I thought I'd give him a head start."

"Well, let's see then." He takes Jackson's painting from me and examines it carefully, looking down his nose through his granny glasses.

Feeling edgy, I say, "He has lots of others, too. This is just the only one I could get my hands on."

"Mighty fine," he says. "How old you say your friend is?"

"He's eighteen."

"His sense of light and shading is somethin' to be reckoned with. He studied art long?"

"I don't believe so," I say. "I reckon it just comes naturally."

"Talented indeed," he says, smiling at me. "I'd say serious potential even. Get him to come on by."

"Thank you!" I say, taking back the picture. "I just knew you'd like it." I head for the door.

"What you say your name was?" he asks.

"It's Savannah," I reply.

"And your friend?"

"Jackson. Jackson Channing."

"I'll be waiting on him," he says, handing me his card.

Before I go, I poke my head into the Living Through Literature auditorium one last time. I reckon the program must have ended. There's not a soul in there.

Oh well, I can't wait to tell Jackson what all the man said. I get home quick as I can with my breathing pulling at me like it is, set the painting back up on the wall, and go for the phone. Forget about letting him stew, this is too dang big.

I get the machine. "Jackson, it's Savannah. I've got something real important to tell you. Call me as soon as you get this." I hang up and wait. But before long, I've got to head out to work.

By Saturday afternoon, Jackson still hasn't called and I'm a wreck, sitting in my room trying to calm my breathing. We haven't talked in four days. He didn't even call after I left that message saying I had something important to tell him. I pushed too hard. I should have given him more room. Now I don't know should I call him again or give him time. I keep pulling on my inhaler, but if I can't get some air soon, I'll have to let Mama in on this. She's going to have to run me up to Mercy for sure. I thought the whole point of taking the durn medicine every day was to avoid this mess. I know that Dr. Jones told me I ought not let myself get all emotional, but it ain't like I get to choose.

I'm writing in my journal when Mama yells at the top of her lungs, "Savannah!"

I don't waste my breath on answering.

"Savannah!" she calls again. "You best come take a gander at this."

I try real hard to act like my breathing is okay. Breath goes in, breath goes out. But as I get out to the living room, I see Mama by the open front door. And standing there on the front step, by Holy God, is Jackson Channing, looking like he done ran the whole way here.

I scream like I've seen a ghost. Mama starts laughing. But Jackson doesn't move. He just stands there looking hurt and worried and breathing nearly as hard as I am. And right there and then, I know he loves me. I can see it pouring right out his eyes. I run and fling my arms around his neck and cry.

"What in the world are you doing here?" I ask.

He kisses my tears away. "I couldn't do it no more," he says. "Greenville, the body shop. I just couldn't take it."

"What about your mama?" I ask, remembering what he said about never cutting out on her.

"She gave me the go. Said you must be sump'n awful special to have such a hold over me."

I can't believe it—one minute worrying I done blown it and now, now . . . "Wait," I say, "you don't mean . . . ?"

He nods and points to his truck, a big old duffel bag in the back.

"You're moving back here?" I shriek.

He nods and wraps me up in his arms.

Mama's got her hand over her mouth like she can't believe it either. "Well come on in. No sense hanging out on the porch with the bugs all afternoon. Let's get this boy something cool to drink. After all, he drove out all this way."

We come inside and sit and drink sweet tea. "Why didn't you say something?" I ask.

He shrugs. "Didn't want to get your hopes up, case it didn't come together. That was why I couldn't tell you what was botherin' me."

"Y'all won't even believe this," Mama says, "but Denny put up the HOUSEPAINTERS NEEDED sign again not two days ago."

"Are you serious?" I say. She nods.

Jackson explains about the deal he made with the Channings to live over their garage. And I finally get to tell him about what the guy at the junior college said. Suddenly, I feel so happy, it seems like I got the opposite of asthma, like I got more air in my lungs than I know what to do with.

28

With Jackson moving back here, I set aside that acceptance letter. Mama pitched a fit the day it was due, but she just doesn't understand. Going up to the mountains can wait till I'm older. There's no rush. Course I still feel a tweak of regret about missing out, but Jackson being here is way bigger.

Come lunchtime, I'm going to ride my bike up to where he's working at so we can eat together. Stef's coming with me so she can finally meet him. I even swallowed my pride and invited Joie. She said she's busy with some girls from school. *Whatever*.

Stef and I ride our bikes up to Jackson's job with a bag of sandwiches and drinks.

"Joie couldn't come. She had plans," I tell Stef on the way.

"She's been hanging out with the cheerleader girls at the mall, you know—Cyndi and Misty and their crowd."

"Cheerleaders? That's who she's calling her 'true friends'? Since when?"

"That night we ditched her," Stef says. "I heard they saw her all upset with too many guys on her hands at the theater and took her under their wing."

"Is that a fact?" I can't hide my surprise. Those girls usually have their noses turned up so high they could rightly drown in a rainstorm.

Jackson waves at us as we reach the site. We set down our bikes and go over, and I introduce him to Stef. For some unknown reason, I feel nervous. I reckon I just want them to like each other.

"I sure have heard a lot about you," Stef says.

"Likewise," says Jackson, though I don't think I've actually spent much of our precious time talking about Stef. I reckon he's being polite, making it sound like I have.

"I hear you got brothers our age." Stef grins.

"Girl!" I say. "What is your problem?"

"What? He's cute. He's got brothers. I've been recently dumped in a manner of speaking. I just thought if they was to come out and visit or what-have-you, I'd want Jackson to know I'm available."

I roll my eyes, but the ice has surely been broken. Jackson laughs, and we all sit down to eat our tuna salad sandwiches with ice cold lemonade.

"I thought you had a boyfriend—Jimmy, wasn't it?" Jackson asks.

I slap his thigh. "I told you what happened when he came to town," I whisper.

"Oh, shoot, I'm sorry. I guess I forgot."

Stef looks forlorn.

"I'm sure you deserve better than him," Jackson says, smoothing things over.

"Damn right she does. You should see this girl dance," I say, aiming to change the subject.

Stef grins. "I *am* a good dancer, I have to admit. Now, Savannah, she slow dances just fine, but soon as the music turns fast she gets all nervous and stiff."

Now I'm slapping *her* thigh. "Shut up!"

They both laugh.

"Maybe you can come to some of our school dances this year," Stef suggests. "They may not be as fancy as the deb balls or cotillions your cousins go to, but they're still fun."

"Maybe." Jackson shrugs.

"We've got plenty of time to worry about that. Let's don't think about school," I groan.

"It ain't but a few weeks away," she says.

I put my hands over my ears. "I can't hear you. Lalalalalala."

Jackson pulls me to him and kisses the top of my head. We finish up eating, and then Stef has to rush off to babysitting and I've got to head to the library. Look at us all, working like grown-ups.

For supper, Mama cooks burgers made with onion soup mix and Tater Tots on the side.

"Jackson," she says, "can you talk some sense into her? That acceptance letter is past due. But if she sends it in quick, they might still take her."

"I know you can't be serious," I say. "*Hello!* Jackson just moved back out here. I can't leave now."

"But he wouldn't want you to miss out on this opportunity. Would you?"

Jackson quits eating. "No, ma'am," he says, and looks at me con-cerned.

"Do we have to talk about this every day?" Dog whines. "I'm sick to death of hearing about it. I'm done. Can I go to Dave's?"

"All right then," Mama sighs. "You want a ride? I need to talk to Gina anyway."

"Why you always got to talk to her?" Dog growls.

"What in the world?" Mama asks. "Excuse me, but she is my best friend and I've barely had time to speak with her lately."

"I don't need no ride and you don't need to be checking up on me all the time."

"Well, excuse me! A simple 'no, thank you,' would have sufficed." Mama shakes her head as Dog takes off.

I stand up. "We're done, too. Can we go down to the beach? It's still light out," I add, just to be on the safe side.

"Please, y'all, just think about that program. This opportunity is too big to pass up."

"Okay, okay," I say, grabbing Jackson's hand and pulling him out the door.

It's still hot as blazes, but at least there's a bit of breeze by the water. Jackson sits down in the sand and looks out there to the sea like I've seen him do before, like he expects to find some answers out that way. He unties his work boots and takes them off.

"You need some flip-flops," I say. But then, I close my mouth and turn to stare out there, too, not wanting to talk, just wanting to sit together quietly.

"How come you don't wanna go?" he asks.

Course I know he's talking about the mountains. "You're finally here," I cry, feeling all sorts of pain welling up in my chest. "You can't actually think I'm gonn' up and leave now!"

"Your mama's right. You cain't pass on this kind of opportunity. How many kids got a letter like that? You cain't just say no."

I shake my head, hating that he wants me to go.

"When I was stuck in Greenville, I thought it might be forever. I thought I might never get to be out here with you, might never get time to paint." He chews on his lip for a few. "You held my dream for me. Your dream was to get outta here, get a chance to go to college, go see those mountains. That dream just up and landed in your lap and you gonn' turn it down? Uh-uh."

"I can't leave you, Jackson."

"Girl, if we ain't strong enough to get through a couple months apart, what good are we? I ain't going nowhere. I'ma be right here when you get back come Christmas, and we'll pick up right where we left off."

"But you came back out here to be with me."

"Yes, I did. But I also came out here to have time to paint, and that's what I'll do while you're away. When you get back, we'll be together."

"How do I know you ain't gonn' be trying no more *experiments*?"

I can see he's hurt by that one. "'Cause you trust me," he says real quiet.

"I don't wanna talk about it no more," I say.

"You don't want to talk?" he teases. "*You*? I never thought I'd hear you say that." Then he's tickling me and we're kissing. And I feel awful desperate.

As we head to the truck, I see Dog down the beach a ways. He's messing around with some bigger boys. I pull Jackson in his direction.

"Dog," I shout. "Where's Dave at?"

He shrugs his shoulders like he can't hear me, then waves, and takes off. He ain't fooling me. I know he heard every word. I'm going to have to have a talk with him.

Mama just will not let it go. She's yelling at me from morning to night about how I'm wasting my chance and destroying my future. Dog suddenly realized if I go he gets the room all to himself, so now he's at my throat all day, too.

"Quit!" I shout. "I'm sick to death of y'all ganging up on me. I'm sorry y'all want me out of here so dang bad, but you're stuck with me. So just hush!"

Mama looks hopeless. I hate disappointing her. I always have. But she just ain't going to win this one.

Part of me feels real sad about letting it go. But the other part is just relieved I don't got to think about it no more. I'll still get to college and to the mountains. It's just postponed is all. It's not like I was expecting to go this soon anyhow. I got my dream-come-true with Jackson moving back here, and one dream ought to be enough for anybody.

On Jackson's day off from work, he calls to say he's got some business to take care of and he's gone all day. In the evening, he takes me to dinner at Eddie's. We go to the movies and out for ice cream. I bug him about going by to see that art guy at the junior college. But he seems tired, so I let it go. I'm just glad we ain't talking about that dag program no more. Now we can settle down and let things get normal.

Me and Jackson are strolling along the beach. I love walking down here with him, the wind blowing my hair all around, the salty moisture on the breeze, the briny smell of the sea, and the bajillions of stars up in the sky, the Milky Way streaking clear across from one end to the other—like magic. We're holding hands and just enjoying being close to one another, up quite a ways now from our usual part of the beach.

"Bought me some paints today," Jackson says like it's no big thing.

"Did you really? Mm-mm. I am proud of you. Canvases, too?" I ask, pleased as punch to see him chasing after that old dream of his.

He smiles, his eyes twinkling in the moonlight. But as we start walking again, we see a bunch of boys up ahead all in a huddle looking like they're up to no good. I'm fixing to turn back the other way when Jackson says, "Wait here."

Now I know he doesn't think I'm crazy enough to stand there by myself when things have suddenly gone and turned all creepy. So I follow right on behind him.

As we get closer, we can see they're all kicking at something, and I'm hoping it ain't some poor beached sea creature, the way they're bashing at it. But I don't smell that awful smell of decaying flesh, so maybe it's just some driftwood they're breaking up for a bonfire or something.

"Get back!" Jackson yells in a voice that sets my teeth on edge. I ain't clear for a minute if he's talking to me or them boys. But we all freeze nonetheless. "What the hell's a matter with y'all? Get out of here 'fore I call the cops!" He lunges like he's going to get them, and they turn tail right quick.

As they disperse, I see what they were kicking—a boy. And as I get closer, I suddenly realize it's Dog down there—all crumpled in a heap.

"Lord God a'mighty!" I scream, dropping to my knees beside him. "Dog! Are you okay? Can you talk? Call an ambulance!" I yell, but there ain't nobody around but us. I've told Mama we need a cell phone for emergencies. I don't care what they cost. Not a priority, my butt! "You were supposed to be at Dave's! Where's he at?" I holler at Dog, then feel bad for yelling when he's so messed up.

He's groaning. His face is swelling, and blood is spilling from his mouth and nose.

Jackson scoops him up like he ain't nothing more than a bundle of twigs and starts hauling him back towards the truck. I follow along, thanking God we decided to walk out this far on the beach tonight, thanking him, too, for Jackson being here to scare them boys off.

My heart is pounding real hard. Jackson's withering under Dog's weight. That boy ain't exactly small. Finally, Jackson sets him down real gentle in the sand.

"Y'all wait here. I'll be right back," he says, and takes off running.

I'm scareder than a bear in a buzzing beehive. Dog is beat up bad, bruised and broken, and I don't know what to do. And the sight of Jackson's back running in the other direction is choking me up.

"Dog? What happened?" I ask as tears prickle my nose. "Can you talk?" He just barely shakes his head. My mind floats right back to the other day when I saw him with those bigger boys at the beach. I should have said something to Mama. I meant to ask Dog about it later. I just forgot.

There's an awful lot of blood coming out his mouth, and his face is turning purple. I hold his head in my lap and cry, praying Jackson is getting help.

But then I see his truck tearing up the beach. He pulls right up beside us. "Get in," he says to me. Then Jackson heaves Dog up and puts his head on my lap again. The three of us are going to be pretty squished up in there with my brother laying down, but that doesn't matter. Jackson covers him with the blanket out of the back of the truck and hops in on my other side. We head straight for Mercy, nobody saying a word.

"Go call your mama," Jackson says, soon as we pull up to Emergency.

I scramble out the driver's side to obey, noting how it's strange being at Mercy and me not being the one in need of help. I ain't got a lick of change on me, so I rush back to the truck to find some. I dig some coins out of the seats and run to the payphones while Jackson gets help for Dog. The orderlies rush out with a gurney.

The phone rings and rings, and I fear I'm going to lose it if she ain't home. Finally she picks up. "Mama!" I cry, feeling like a little kid, relieved to hear her voice.

"What's wrong?" she asks, knowing by my tone it's serious.

"We're at Mercy," I say.

Before I can explain, she says, "Damnit! Did you forget your inhaler again? It's been too much excitement. I been saying it to Denny over and over. It's just too much—"

"Mama!" I cut her off. "It ain't me. It's Dog." And I realize how strange that is, for once it ain't me causing all the commotion and worry.

Dead silence hangs on the line. Then she goes, "Dog? Whatcha mean?"

I can feel my tears lining up again. "He got beat up real bad. He's bleeding and bruised."

"But he's at Gina's," Mama says in a small, confused voice. Then it finally hits her that maybe he's not. "We'll be right there."

Jackson and I sit side by side in the metal scoop chairs in the waiting room. I've got Dog's blood all over my khaki shorts, and it's all over Jackson's T-shirt, too. There's a couple of not-too-clean-looking fellas watching the TV, a young guy sleeping across three chairs, some hairy dude looking like he's fixing to puke, and an old lady with blue hair sitting all proper with her hands in her lap like she's at church.

DC and Mama come racing in and get taken back to where Dog's at.

"He'll be okay," Jackson says after a while.

I nod. "Thanks for toting him," I say. Did you ever notice how silence feels so ominous in a hospital? "What you think went on back there?" I ask just to fill the hole.

He doesn't answer at first. "Got in with the wrong crowd, I reckon."

"Why wadn't he with Dave like he told Mama he was gonn' be? Why didn't Gina call if he left without Dave? He must be embarrassed as hell, us finding him like that, though he ought rightly to be grateful." I'm still rambling on like a crazy person when DC comes out.

"Y'all okay?" he asks us.

We nod. "How is he?" I ask.

"He'll be a'ight. Got a broken nose, a black eye, and a missing tooth. They gonn' do some X-rays, see if'n his ribs or his arm is broke and check out his internal organs." He pauses. "That boy is jacked up but good."

"We found him at the beach," I explain. "A bunch of boys were kicking him." I'm getting all emotional again. "Jackson scared 'em off and carried him to the truck."

DC puts out his hand, and Jackson shakes it. "You done good, son," DC says.

For the first time in my life, my brother has to stay over in the hospital and I don't. It is a strange feeling. I've got to admit, there were times when I was younger when I wished it was him that had to stay, that I'd be the one leaving with Gina. But now that it's happening, it doesn't feel right at all. Me, I know how to handle being stuck in this awful place. But Dog doesn't know a thing about it, and I find myself wishing I could take it away for him. All this time, I never realized how much it must hurt Mama to worry for me like this. I reckon even Dog gets concerned, though he doesn't show it too often.

After a while, a policeman approaches us.

"I understand you two were witnesses," he says.

"Yes, sir," I reply, and recount for him everything I can remember about what we saw at the beach.

"That how you saw it?" he asks Jackson, like he doesn't believe me.

"Yes, sir," Jackson says.

"You got anything to add?" the policeman asks him.

"No, sir," he replies.

"Y'all recognize those boys?" He eyes us like he's expecting us to lie or something.

You can bet if I knew any of them I wouldn't hesitate to tell him. But sadly, I didn't recognize a single one, though I'd wager Dog probably knew a few.

"All right, then," he says, like he's giving up on us. "Unless somebody can I.D. those boys, we won't be able to press charges."

Truth is, it was dark; they weren't familiar; I was sick with worry over Dog. I doubt I'd even be able to pick them out of a lineup.

The cop swaggers off to flirt with a nurse, case closed.

Mama comes out to tell us to go on home. But she looks terrible shook up, so we decide to all stay out in the waiting area ruther than leaving her here by herself. It's uncomfortable as hell in them hard chairs, but I doze off from time to time, dreaming of Dog getting the nebulizer and struggling to breathe and being poked with needles and me hiding behind the curtain letting him take my medicine.

In the morning, DC sends Jackson home to sleep. Before Jackson leaves, Mama thanks him over and over and invites him to come by for Sunday dinner, which seems a mite unusual seeing as we usually just have sandwiches or what-have-you on Sundays. Then when Dog gets released, DC drives him and Mama and me on home and helps get Dog situated in the bed. He's got his arm in a cast, taped-up ribs, a bandaged nose, and a black-and-blue eye. He's on a whole mess of painkillers, so he goes out like a light. Then DC leaves. Me and Mama sit at the table drinking coffee. She looks awful worn.

"I'm sorry," I say.

"Whatever for?" Mama asks, looking up from where she's been staring into her mug.

I shrug. "I been so absorbed with my own affairs, I hadn't paid attention to the fact that something was up with him." Mama still appears confused. "It's always been my job, looking out for him. I neglected it. I'm real sorry." And Lord do I feel like my insides are near about ready to gush out of me like water from a busted hydrant.

Mama shakes her head. "He's old enough to be looking out for his own self. And you"—she sighs real heavy—"you ain't really his keeper, Vannah, no more than he is yours. I shouldn't have put that on you. If anyone's to blame, it's me. I should have been checking in with Gina. I've been so wrapped up with Denny, I just let it slide. He told me how y'all rescued Dog."

"It was Jackson," I say. "I didn't do nothing."

"You were there for him. You called me. Y'all did good."

I don't want to upset her, but I can't seem to hold my tongue. "How come he wadn't at Gina's?"

Quiet little tears roll down Mama's cheeks, making me wish I'd have kept my mouth shut. "I called her from the hospital. I lit into her like you wouldn't believe." And she laughs through her tears. But then she looks real serious again. "Gina said she thought I knew Dog and Dave had quit hanging out a week or so back, said they had some kind of fight, got ill with each other and hadn't spoken a word since. She thought I hadn't called her lately 'cause I was mad at her over it. I didn't have the heart to tell her I been so busy with Denny and all that I just hadn't had the time to call."

"So where does Dog go every day?" I wonder out loud.

"According to Gina, Dave and Dog started hanging out with some boys from St. Bartholomew's earlier in the summer. Course she didn't know about it at the time."

"The school for juvies?" I ask, appalled.

"Come on, now. They're not 'juvies,'" Mama says. "They're troubled, but, yes, they did go there during the school year."

"Dog!" I exclaim.

"Apparently, Dave got scared off a week or two ago and backed out. But Dog just ditched him and kept on with those boys. I believe he's learnt his lesson."

"What about the cops? Are they gonn' go after those boys?"

Mama sighs. "They say they can only press charges if Dog identifies them. I don't know how likely that is to happen. If I know Dog, he's gonn' keep his mouth shut. School will be starting up in a couple of weeks, and he ain't gonn' be out my sight until then."

I put my hands over my ears. "Don't talk about it. Summer is *not* ending, not ever."

Mama laughs a little. I reckon she is seriously overtired. "Can't put a hold on time, darlin'. It marches on whether you like it or not."

I lay my head on my arms, wishing it wasn't so.

29

"Savannah, get me a Coke!" Dog calls from where he's laying up on the couch.

Get me a Coke, fix me some cheese grits, find me the remote. I am sick to death of that boy and his demands. I wish he'd go on and get well so he can get out my hair. With Mama busier than a one-legged man in a butt-kicking contest, trying to prepare this unexplained traditional Sunday dinner, and Dog, ornery as ever, making requests every five minutes, I'm fixing to lose my mind.

"Vannah, check and see if the potatas are cooked off for me, please," Mama calls in a strained voice.

"Since when do we have a big ol' Sunday dinner anyhow?" I ask.

Mama holds out a wooden spoon in a threatening manner. "Looky here, I thought it'd be a nice way to say thank you to Jackson. I could sure use a little more help and a little less lip outta you, missy."

It is sweet of her and all. I just reckon Jackson would have been as happy with burgers and fries. But I ain't going to rain on her parade. I check the potatoes and set the table for five. She sure is cooking up a feast. She even bought a big old ham like it's Christmas or something. She's doing collards and mashed potatoes with gravy, corn on the cob, fresh baked biscuits and green bean casserole—the kind with the little fried onions on top. She even made an apple pie and a Jell-O mold for dessert.

"You coulda waited till I can eat it, too," Dog whines. He can't have nothing but soft foods since them boys kicked him in the mouth.

"You can have some mashed potatas. And who you think I made the Jell-O for?"

Dog whimpers.

By the time DC and Jackson arrive, Mama and I have got the table set up with a feast fit for a king. Even though we put a place for Dog, he ain't up to coming to the table. Mama brings him a tray on the couch with the mushy stuff. He looks like he could just cry. Ham's his *favorite* favorite and we don't hardly ever get to have it.

I sit beside Jackson, and DC sits by Mama. We have ourselves one hell of a meal, laughing and joking, everybody feeling easy and comfortable. It seems so strange and also so perfect. The men even help us clear the table. Then they go hang with Dog and watch a baseball game on TV.

"I sure wish I could have talked you into that program," Mama says as we're washing up the dishes.

"What's done is done," I say, hoping to put a lid on it.

"But it's what you've always wanted—travel, seeing the Blue Ridge Mountains, a chance at college—it don't make no sense, Van."

My stomach starts in to aching. "It just came at the wrong time is all. I reckon it wasn't meant to be. I haven't given up anything, though, not really. I'll still get to college. I'll go check out the mountains, too. You'll see. You worry too much," I say, trying to seem cheerful as I put aside the last of the dishes.

Mama sighs real heavy. That old sound effect of disappointment always hits me right in my gut.

30

Since Dog's healing up pretty good, he's up and around and even hanging out with Dave again. Mama's got him on a strict punishment, though. He can't leave the house without adult supervision. Lucky for him, Gina's out of work, so she comes by and gets him.

Mama sure laid into him about all the lying. That boy was getting to where he didn't know the truth from a cow pile. Mama said she catches him lying again, he just may find himself going to school with them boys what beat him up. She's thinking she might send him to St. Bart's! I reckon he won't be lying anytime soon. He begged Mama not to press charges, fearing those boys might come after him. So he knows he best keep his nose clean.

I'm relieved that for the last little bit of summer, everything is just like I want it to be. I mean, sure it'd be nice if Jackson didn't have to work all day, but we get to spend near about every evening together and his days off. Plus, I like reading and swimming and biking on my own. I'm getting big chunks of my SAT workbook done. Stef comes by and visits me while I'm working at the library most days, and we've even laid out at the beach a few times. We saw Joie down there one day in an itty-bitty bikini with the cheerleader girls. They were treating her like the hired help, but she didn't seem to mind. We tried to wave her over, but she just ignored us. I reckon she's thrilled them girls are including her in any fashion. She was even practicing cheers with them. I wonder if she'll go out for the squad.

I roll my butt out of bed and meander into the kitchen to drink some orange juice. I see the postman out the window, so I step outside to bring in the mail.

A shocking feeling of ice in my gut tears right through me as I take the letters out of the box and find a thick packet addressed to me from the dean of the University of North Carolina. My skin prickles. What could they possibly want from me now? I sit down on the front steps, trying to drum up my courage to open the envelope.

Real slow, I tear it open, one little bit at a time.

Welcome! it says. Welcome? What in the hell?

It is my great pleasure to welcome you to the UNC-Asheville Program for Promising High School Students.

No. Uh-uh. I've got to look away. I can't read no more. I'm fixing to cry. My breath is turning shallow. The world is crashing down on me. What is going on here? I never sent in that acceptance.

Dropping all the mail on the front steps, I run inside, slamming the screen door on the way. I rush into my room and start throwing stuff around, looking for that letter I never mailed. When I'm sure it ain't there, I call Mama at work. By now I am full on sobbing. "Did . . . you . . . do . . . this?" I ask her, trying to get air into my lungs between my words and tears.

"Darlin', what's wrong? Settle down and use your inhaler. Do you need me to come home?"

"Why . . . did . . . you . . . send . . . in . . ." I'm sniffling and snuffling and generally making a scene.

"Savannah. Listen to me. I can't understand what you're talking about. The only thing I know is you have got to simmer down so you can breathe. I want you to hang up the phone. I'm coming straight home. Just breathe, you hear?"

I let the phone fall to the floor and try my best to settle down. But it ain't working. Why would she do this when I made it clear it wasn't what I wanted? How dare she decide for me? I can't leave, I just can't. She can't make me, neither. I won't go. I just won't. My breath isn't coming so good. Even my thoughts feel like they're drowning.

Mama comes racing in, DC a few steps behind her. They tote me off to Mercy. All that crying has sent me over the edge.

Mama scribbles away in her notebook by my bedside. DC must be out in the ER waiting room.

I hold the mask off my face so I can talk. "Why'd you do it?" I ask, hurt but calm.

She shakes her head. "Denny found the letter on the front steps when we came to get you. It wadn't me, sugar. And it wadn't him neither. That just leaves one person far as I can see."

At that very minute, Jackson walks in, his clothes all covered in paint. He takes my hand, strokes my hair. "You okay?" he asks. As he wipes my tears away with his thumb, I see Mama sliding out of the room.

I don't even care about the fact that I'm sitting there in the raggedy old shorts and T-shirt I always sleep in, my hair likely sticking up with bedhead. I repeat my question to him. "Why'd you do it?"

He looks down at his feet for a moment, then straight into my eyes. "I kept thinking 'bout how you filled out that application for me when you found the yella sign, and then how you took my paintin' down to the guy at the college. I figured one turn deserves another."

I shake my head. "When?"

"On my day off. 'Member I said I had some business to attend to? The day before that I'd called up the people at the program and told 'em there'd been a problem at home that had prevented you from sending in your letter on time. At first they said it was too late. So I asked 'em if they'd given away your spot yet, and they said no. I offered to fax the letter over to 'em right then. But they insisted on having the original. And they said offers were going out the next day, my day off, to the replacement students. I told 'em they'd have your acceptance by the time their office opened that morning."

"How?" I ask.

"I drove through the night."

"To *Asheville*?"

He nods. "I stopped for a catnap about three a.m., made it to their doorstep by seven. Then I just waited for 'em to open at nine. I figured I'd come all that way, I wadn't gonn' risk just slipping it through the mail slot. After I handed it in and knew it was all taken care of, I went and slept in the truck for a while, then drove back in time to meet you for dinner."

"I can't believe you went to all that trouble." I turn my head to look out the window, feeling all choked up inside.

He tips my face back to him real gentle. "You hold my dream. I hold yours," he says.

Now what can you say to that?

"What you scared of?" he asks.

I start thinking about how bad off my breathing had got the last few days before he moved back down here. "Maybe I can't breathe without you."

He takes my hand in his and sits quiet for a minute. Then he says, "You remember you told me about the tornada you were named after?"

I nod.

"Just like it, you got as much strength and wind as you need. Alls you got to do now is to know that you can do without me or your daddy or anybody. You got to know you can breathe all on your own."

Something inside me sort of crumbles right then. Like I know he's right, that I got to find out if I can breathe on my own, be my own cure, else someday I'm going to find myself laying on a couch for twelve years waiting for somebody to come and rescue me.

31

*L*uckily, I get released from Mercy. I just got myself over-excited is all. When we get home, Jackson and DC stay outside unloading some bags of mulch from DC's truck. Mama and I go on in the house.

"Mama," I tell her, "maybe I might go on and check out the mountains after all."

"Praise Jesus!" she shouts, clapping her hands together. "Did Jackson talk you into it? I just knew that boy was one of the good ones."

I think back to her little manifesto of earlier this summer and wonder when exactly it was that she changed her mind. But there are more important matters at hand just now.

"There's still one thing we haven't figured on: how we gonn' afford it?" I ask, not quite looking at her, not wanting to bring up an issue that might embarrass her. "I saved up some money from working at the library, but it ain't nearly enough."

"I thought about that quite a bit," she says. "If only I'd a managed to put money away for y'all's college, we'd be Johnny on the spot." She sighs real heavy. "Two thousand is a lot. But I believe if I increase my hours working for Denny and waitress on the side, we can pull it off."

DC walks in and sits down at the table, sweat dripping off his forehead. "Listen here y'all," he says. "I ain't trying to play the hero or nothing. But if Savannah's gonn' go, I'ma pay for her program."

"Are you serious?" I ask, amazed that he would do that for me.

He nods.

But then dead silence creeps into the corners of the room.

"That won't be necessary," Mama says, turning red, as she hands him a glass of sweet ice tea. "I appreciate your offer, I do. But we'll manage just fine."

"Mama," I say real soft, "maybe we should think about this. DC is making a real nice offer."

She turns on me. "Don't start. If I want to work extra, that don't concern nobody but me."

"Course it do," Denny retorts. "It concerns us all. You think Savannah wants to think of you having to work your butt off for her? You think I want you out at some grease pit every evening? What about Dog? Who's gonn' look after him? Look here, doll, I know you been on your own a long time and you used to managing come hell or high water, and I have admired that strength in you since the day we met, but things is different now."

"Denny," Mama interrupts. "I can't take no handouts."

And I see how much it pains her to feel like she ain't done well enough by us to make things work.

"This ain't no handout! Is 'at what you think? That I'm some sort of good Samaritan wanting to help some poor needy souls?" He shakes his head like he's hurt and confused both. Then he goes, "Ain't nobody *ever* treated you right? Ever shown you sump'n called *generosity*?"

Mama looks like she's fixing to cry. I take her hand. "It ain't pity," I promise her real quiet.

"Pity?" DC storms, slamming down his glass of ice tea on the table. "Is 'at what you think? Is it, Porsha?"

"DC," I say, "what are you getting so mad about?" Suddenly he ain't helping the situation one bit.

"Mad? Here I hoped your mama might one day see me as family, might be starting to believe I'm somebody she can count on, somebody she cares for, and now, come to find out, I'm just as much an outsider as I ever been. Ain't nothin' changed for her." His veins are pulsing in his neck, his face blood red.

"Now, Denny, that just ain't true," Mama starts. "You know I care for you. I do consider you, well, you are becoming family. It's just that this here's a lot of money, and I don't want to feel like you got a hold over me."

"A hold?" he demands.

Mama tries to backpedal. "I want to know we're together because we care for each other, not because I feel beholden."

"What if'n I say this here's between me and Savannah and it ain't got a thing to do with you?" he asks, all huffy.

"Ain't no grown man gonn' be handing my daughter two thousand dollars," Mama warns.

"Maybe there's a scholarship or something through school," I say, wanting to ease the tension.

DC glares at Mama. "You are dearly hurting my feelings, Porsha."

She goes over and takes his hand. "I ain't used to nobody giving me something this big for no good reason."

"No good reason?" he storms. "How about a reason called love? That good enough for you? I love you, Porsha. Let me help. Please."

Mama just stares at him like he's some kind of alien from Mars. I'm frozen still in my spot waiting to see what she's going to do. Then, next thing I know, they're kissing and crying, and I guess that means I got the money.

Jackson comes in with Dog trailing at his heels. My brother takes one look at Mama and DC and snaps, "Well ain't that romantical."

"Dog," Mama warns.

I'm about to yell at him to give her a break, but Jackson steps in.

"Hey," he says real neutral, "be glad for your mama. She deserves some happiness, don't she?"

And right away I can see Dog soften, like he finally saw something from her view instead of his own. Now why it took Jackson to make him see, I don't know. But there it is.

DC says, "Savannah's going to the mountains."

"Yee-haw!" Dog yells.

I catch Jackson's eye, and he looks real proud. It still hurts something fierce to think about leaving. But like he said, it won't be for too long.

Mama starts fixing food for everybody, and DC goes, "Savannah, can I ask you sump'n?"

"Sure," I reply.

"You never did tell me why you call me DC—like I'm some sort of citified Yankee from up by the Mason-Dixon Line. Can't be from my name, 'cause what would the C stand for? You know my name is Dennis Johnson. And I ain't never told you my middle name, but it's Darryl. So what's the C?"

I blush till my eyeballs go red. "It's nothing," I say.

But of course now everybody wants to know, and they won't let up.

"Fine. The C is for caterpillar, okay? 'Cause of your mustache. It reminds me of a big old hairy caterpillar."

"Savannah!" Mama chides. "I never! Mind your manners."

But DC just laughs. "Coulda been worse," he says.

32

With little more than a week to go before I take off, I feel like somebody has mashed down the fast-forward button, like there just ain't enough time left.

I had my appointment with Dr. Tamblin. Everything checked out okay. I'm going to have to keep on taking the daily meds, but he believes I'll find it easier to breathe up there in the mountains, which doesn't make a lick of sense to me, 'cause as I've been reading up on it, sounds like there's less air up there. But I reckon he's the doctor. He ought rightly to know.

I got a letter from my roommate-to-be, Rae Ann something or another. She seems nice enough. She said her bed comforter is blue in case I want to match. I don't. But I sure am glad she didn't say it was pink with princesses on it or some such nonsense. She's from Hendersonville, so she won't be traveling too far at all. She can even go home on the weekends. I wonder if Jackson might could drive up there to visit me once in a while. Course he'd have to save up enough money to pay for someplace to stay. I don't reckon they'd allow him up in the dorms. Or maybe I could at least come home for Thanksgiving. Four months sure does sound like a long haul.

Stef is pissed as all hell that I'm going. I mean, not for real. She's happy for me, but she's just wishing I'd be there to gossip with at lunch and to sit with in some of her classes. Truth be told, I'd have been in AP for half my courses and she's in on-level, so we'd be lucky just to get our electives together. I wonder will she go and make a whole new batch of friends while I'm gone? And how will she feel with me away and Joie ignoring her? Although, truth be told, Stef says the cheerleaders are already losing interest in Joie. I can't worry over it all, just have to wait and see how it goes.

Meanwhile, I best spend my energy on getting my stuff together. It ain't easy finding what I need under all of Dog's mess. I start by digging my way through the closet for some of my favorite books.

"Dog! Come get your crap out of my side of the closet!" I yell, fed up with it.

"He ain't here," Mama calls back.

I go out to the living room, glad for an excuse to step out of that mess. "Where's he at?" I ask, annoyed.

Mama's laying on the couch, her eyes closed. "Jackson took him up to the site when he left earlier on, thought he'd show Dog what all they're doing."

"Why?" I ask, not sure I like the idea of my brother hanging out with my boyfriend.

"Dog's been stuck in the house so much, I reckon Jackson was just trying to be friendly."

"Huh." I still don't get it.

"Dog may have convinced me not to press charges against those boys, but I intend to keep him supervised when he goes out for a while," Mama says. "I reckon Jackson felt sorry for him. Anyhow, you need some help?"

I do, but she looks tired. "That's all right," I say.

"Come on. Ain't but a few more days I'm gonn' be around to lend you a hand. You can be all on your own once you get there."

I can't help but feel glad she wants to. It's lonely packing up like this, trying to decide what to take and what not to. She helps me move Dog's stuff out of the way.

"You sure are gonn' be surrounded by guys with me gone," I say.

"Lord, you're right," she says, folding Dog's jeans. "I'd better set myself up some time with Gina or I may never see a romantic comedy again."

"Oh, hush. You know DC'll take you to any picture you want."

She sits back against the wall looking pleased.

"You love him?" I ask.

She nods. "He sure has grown on me." We both laugh. "At first, he just came on so darn strong, looking at me like I was the Virgin Mary or something. But, like all men, he showed his true colors down the line. Turned out, I like them colors just fine."

"He treats you real good," I say.

"He sure does, hon. 'Bout like you and Jackson."

My heart fills right up to the top hearing her say that, having her treat us as a real grown-up couple. "I love him something fierce."

"I know you do, sugar. Part of me wants to remind you that you're young yet, not to get your hopes up. Hold on now, don't get upset. There's the other part says to just shut up. Y'all have certainly proven me wrong time and again. And I can tell y'all truly have something special."

I dive right into her arms and hug her but good. I believe I just now realized how much I'm going to miss her.

Jackson and Dog come straggling in just in time for supper.

"Where y'all been at?" I ask, glaring at the football in Dog's hands. The cast on his arm is all muddy and starting to tear.

"Dog helped me run a few errands. So I tossed the football with him some down at the beach."

I've got to admit I am mad. What's he doing tossing a football with Dog when we ain't got but a few more days together?

"You don't own him," Dog grumbles.

"Shut up!" I yell. "While you were out playing ball, I been digging through your mess all afternoon! And I'm just sick of it!"

Jackson comes right over and kisses me real gentle, brushing his thumb across my cheek. "Them errands was for a surprise for you. Don't be mad."

I settle, but I ain't appeased. We sit down to eat, and I feel sunk in my worries. I ain't at all sure I want to leave. Meanwhile, Jackson and Dog are cutting up and cracking jokes. I feel left out. Is it weird to worry about your brother stealing your boyfriend? Not like in *that* way. I just don't want them to get to be too good of friends. I reckon I'm just jealous.

I don't find out my surprise right away. But on my last day at home, Jackson acts nervous and excited. And believe you me, it's catching. He's got me all on edge.

He picks me up at the house around suppertime. Mama's grinning like she knows all about it. Me and Jackson get in the truck and drive and drive until he pulls up on a real pretty piece of beach. It's wide and flat and the waves are rolling in real gentle. He takes a duffel bag from the back of the truck and leads me to a spot of his choosing.

He sets out a tartan picnic blanket I reckon he got from his aunt. I sit down feeling all fluttery. He takes out two of them fancy champagne glasses—you know the tall skinny ones? I always wondered how folks in the movies manage to drink from them tiny openings without their noses getting in the way. Course neither one of us is old enough for champagne, so he fills them up with Sprite. He sets those down in the sand and unloads from his bag a beautiful picnic supper. There's barbecued shrimp, corn salad, and potato salad.

"Where did you get all this?" I ask him.

"My aunt made the corn salad and your mama made the potato salad, but I fixed the shrimp myself." He's blushing proud.

"Mm-mm. I am sincerely impressed," I say. I can see his bag ain't empty yet. "What else you got in there?"

"Don't be nosy." He smiles and holds up the champagne glasses. I take one and he says, "To following dreams."

I clink his glass, but suddenly there's a big ol' lump in my throat and I ain't sure that Sprite's even going to have room to go down. But he holds my hand and we drink to our dreams.

"Now that you're staying down here, you really ought to call that dude at the junior college," I say, thinking he might just need a little push to get going towards his own aspirations.

"I was just fixin' to tell you about that." He starts in to blushing. "I went by there with a few more of my pieces. He wanted to show 'em at the student gallery."

"Jackson! That's amazing!" I cry.

He shrugs. "'Cept he can only show students' work there."

My heart sinks for him. It just doesn't seem fair. There must be some way around it.

"So he got me to sign up for some evening art classes at the college." He peeks up at me like he knows I'm going to explode. And of course I do.

I knock him down with a hug and gush over him going after his own heart's desire. I just can't get over how happy I feel for him, as if it was my own wish coming to light. I near about smother him with hugs and kisses. Two dreams coming through all at once, seems near about too good to be true, which makes me nervous. Finally, we settle down and start to eat. The sauce is nice, but the shrimp is a bit rubbery.

"I reckon I overcooked it," he says.

"No, it's good," I tell him. I'm just so tickled that he went to all this trouble. He brought real plates and forks and everything—no paper or plastic. And we've got most of the beach to ourselves, except for a few beachcombers down the way.

He pulls out Hello Dollies for dessert. Some folks call them seven-layer bars, but I prefer the name Mama always used when she'd make them when me and Dog were little.

"Don't tell me you bake, too?" I ask him.

"My Aunt June made those," he confesses. They're awful good.

"I am so proud of you going after that dream of yours. Maybe we do get to choose after all, huh?" I say, nudging him on the shoulder.

He smiles like he might be a little embarrassed for doubting me in the first place.

"Wait till Mama hears about this. You tell your own ma?" I ask him.

"Not yet. She don't think paintin' is serious work," he says.

"You should tell her just the same. I know she'd be proud."

He digs a hole in the sand, sticks a candle in it to protect the flame from the breeze and lights it. Then he hands me a present—a small rectangular box wrapped a bit haphazardly in red paper.

I cover my mouth. "You didn't have to do that," I say.

"Go on and open it," he encourages.

Real slow, I tear off the paper, wanting to make this moment last. I hesitate before opening the box. Oh my word! It's a delicate gold chain with a pretty little gold heart hanging on it.

"That way you'll always know my heart's with you," he says, and he's blushing for real.

Law! I reckon I've got to forgive him for hanging out with Dog my last week at home. I don't know what to say. I have all these feelings inside me—ecstatic joy and fierce pain and profound love all mixed together. I wish he could just sense what's going on inside of me without me having to struggle for words that couldn't possibly even touch it.

"Wait here a minute," he says. He grabs his bag and runs a short distance down the beach and next thing I know, he's setting off fireworks—gold and green and red—just for me! And I say a prayer real quick just to make sure I don't go and wake up.

33

*A*ugust 30 arrives. Somehow it crept up on us, and I ain't at all ready. I mean, my bags are packed and all, but I just ain't ready. Laying in bed for the last few minutes, I wonder, what if my breathing goes all topsy-turvy when I'm on my own? What if I do need Jackson for real? But I can hear what he'd say already: *Can't nobody do your breathing for you, girl. It's time for you to see you can do it your own self.*

Mama comes in just then to get me up. "How you feeling?" she asks.

"Terrible," I say.

"Come on, now, it ain't so bad." She sits on the edge of my bed, pushes my hair out of my face.

"Thank you for everything." My voice is thick with feeling.

"I'm real happy for you," she says, her voice trembly, "and proud to boot. First one in the family to actually make it onto the college track, mm mm mm."

"Hate to interrupt this little love fest," Dog moans from his bed, "but can y'all shut up? I'm trying to sleep."

Mama and I just laugh.

After I shower and get dressed, I come out for breakfast, though I can't imagine eating nothing. My stomach is all tied up in knots. My eyes nearly pop out of my head as I see DC walking through the door—minus his mustache! He actually looks sort of decent without it.

"Whatcha think?" DC asks.

"Not bad," I say.

"Guess you can't exactly call me DC no more, huh?"

I laugh. "You may have shaved off that hairy caterpillar, but you always gonn' be DC to me."

I hug him real hard, knowing it's thanks to him I'm going at all. He takes my stuff out to Jackson's truck, which has just pulled up in the drive.

"Dog, get out here and come say bye to your sister," Mama yells.

"Bye!" Dog shouts back from the bedroom.

"Dogwood Booker Brown!" Mama yells.

He knows he's in trouble now. He ambles out of the room in his boxer shorts, his eyes all squinched up. The cast on his arm is looking ratty, but his bruises have faded.

"See you, Savannah," he says, and actually manages to sound sort of somber.

"Don't go taking over the room," I say. "I'm only gone till Christmas." I'm afraid to even think what that poor room is going to look or smell like when I get back.

Jackson, who has just walked in, says, "You go on ahead and make as a big a mess as you want, Dog. That room is yours."

I swat Jackson on the arm. "Thanks for backing me up."

He smiles. "Denny and I are gonn' build you on an extra bedroom and an extra bathroom, too. With me and him coming by all the time, one bathroom ain't enough."

"Are you serious?" I squeal. I look from his face to Mama's to DC's, and I see that they are!

"When you come back in December," Jackson promises, "you gonn' have your very own bedroom. What color you want it to be?"

Without a moment's hesitation, I say, "I want a mural. I want your art splashed across my walls. You surprise me." And I can see he's pleased. Just think, no more NASCAR posters, no more junk all over the floor, no more stinky socks or sweaty clothes on my bed. My very own room! Now I admit there's a part of me wondering if that extra bathroom is 'cause DC might be hoping to move in here one day. If that feeling I had of them being in it for the long haul is true, I reckon he will.

"Y'all better head out, or Savannah's gonn' miss her train," Mama warns. She hugs me real hard and starts to cry.

I can't believe this is even happening. I stand at the threshold, afraid to take that first step, my breathing getting just a mite crunchy. But I take a couple puffs off my inhaler, steel my nerves, and step outside.

Mama, DC, and even Dog stand on the steps waving till we're out of sight. Now me and Jackson have got our last two hours together till we get to the station. To be honest, I'm scareder than that canary caught by that cat, I tell you what.

❧ ❧ ❧

The car ride seems to go by awful quick. We hardly talk at all, just listen to music on the radio. He drives with one hand and holds mine with the other. Strange that this here might be our last chance to talk in person for four whole months, and both of us are all clammed up. Course Jackson ain't never been big on talking and me, well, I'm just too durn nervous to open my mouth. As we get further from home, I scoot closer to him, lean my head on his shoulder, try to memorize the way he smells—like the beach and paint—and the way he feels— soft, yet strong and solid, warm. In fact, come to find out, what he feels like is home.

"Jackson," I say, swallowing hard, fixing to tell him to go on and turn us around.

But he squeezes my leg and says, "You gonn' be just fine, Savannah."

So I hold my tongue.

Before I know it, we're pulling up to the train station and my heart starts in to beating like a hamster on a running wheel. Jackson gets my luggage out of the back and sets it on the curb. I'm still sitting up in the front, unmoving. He comes over and opens my door and offers me a hand down. I take a couple of deep breaths, throw my backpack over my shoulder, and join him. We hug real tight and kiss each other sort of quick what with all them people around.

Jackson says, "I got sump'n I want to say to you."

You can bet I'm all ears now.

He takes a folded-up piece of paper out of his pocket and grins sort of sheepishly. "I was afraid I'd get nervous and forget it."

Suddenly I'm grinning ear to ear just at the thought that he done took the time to think about what he wanted to say to me before I left, and then I'm wishing I'd done something for him, too.

I grab at the heart pendant hung around my neck, making sure it's still there.

He looks at his paper, then at me. "Savannah . . ." He hesitates, clearing his throat, looking embarrassed. "I love you 'cause you're smart and funny and different, 'cause you seem full of magic. Somehow, you got the whole world in your pocket, make the stars seem within reach." He smiles nervously and crumples the paper in his hand. "You go on after your dream, now. I'll be waiting for you right here when you get back. I know you gonn' have a real great time." He hangs his head for a moment, like he's too shy to look at me all the sudden.

Sheesh! Can you imagine a guy sounding all poetic, pouring his heart out like that? I am at a loss for words. I just cry and kiss him and bury my head in his shoulder. My eyes catch sight of his shoes and Lordy be . . . he's wearing a brand-new pair of flip-flops! I've been so anxious all morning, I hadn't even noticed.

They make an announcement for my train, and I know it's time to go. Painful as it is to be the one walking away, I pick up my luggage, hoist my backpack, and step forward. Once I get settled in my seat, I can see him out the window. I wave, and he smiles at me. I believe he might have even just wiped a tear! This here is one of the hardest things I've ever had to do, and you know what, my breathing ain't too bad, a little clunky is all.

As the train lurches into motion and begins to pull out of the station, my heart jumps right on up in my throat as I think back on all the ways my life has transformed in one single solitary summer and all the changes going to be waiting for me when I get back.

Then up out of nowhere comes one of my too-true feelings. Even though everything is going all right, the sense I get is that what's on the way is even better. I imagine me and Jackson strolling down the beach together when I get home. Only the me in my mind has changed somehow—in a way only I can discern. It's in the way I hold myself, in the tilt of my head, in the easy swell of my lungs, 'cause what's different is who I am inside. That new me there has a knowing this me here doesn't quite have a grasp on yet, a knowing that comes from scaling my own mountain, a knowing that comes from breathing—all on my own.

Acknowledgments

My dream of becoming a published author took many years to realize. There were times along the way when I lost hope and was ready to give up. Luckily, I have always had people in my life who believed in me and kept me going.

My thank you's begin and end with my family: to my husband, Oded, who dreamed my dreams with me, helped me find my way out when my chosen path was no longer working, pushed me on when I didn't know if I could continue, served as my medical consultant, and read so many drafts of books with not a single car chase or battle scene; to my daughter, Maya, for reading all my manuscripts, offering helpful guidance, and for her profoundly loving and joyful spirit; to my son, Jonah, for being patient and understanding when I took time to write, for his deeply caring nature, and for always making me smile; to them all for their unwavering belief.

To my parents, Arna Brandel and Bob Lefkowitz, thank you for giving me permission and freedom to believe in my dreams and for providing me with loving support every step of the way. And to my siblings, David, Noah, Mara, and Josh for their encouragement and for being a constant loving presence in my life. Thank you to Jeanne Tsai for believing in me, even when I couldn't believe in myself, and for always being there. To Shawn Register, for reading an early draft, serving as my Southern consultant, and keeping me focused on the positive.

Thank you also to my writing group, facilitated by the ever inspiring Susanne West and "the regulars"—Fred Anlyan and Carrie Vanderwagen. And to the other writing teachers who helped me find my voice—Janell Moon, Lillian Cunningham, and Thea Sullivan. And to my first writing group at Kai One Place, Kailua, Oahu, for their faith in me. I would also like to thank Tom Barron for believing in me and reminding me to never give up. And John Coie, my undergraduate mentor, who upon hearing of my decision to leave the PhD program in psychology, said to me, "Take the time to find your place in this world and feel good about it." That is my wish for every one of you reading this.

And then, of course, there are the people who made my dream a reality: My deep gratitude goes to my agent, Leigh Feldman, for giving wings to my dream and seeing Savannah's potential. To Joy Peskin, the most amazing editor, for helping me to make this story whole and complete and for being so available, responsive, and patient throughout this process. And thank you to Regina Hayes and everyone else at Viking Children's Books for all their work and support. My infinite gratitude to you all.

Of course, I can't end this without a thank you to Savannah Georgina Brown for jumping into my head and telling me her story.

And, as I said, in the end as in the beginning is always my family. I love you, my special little one; sister of my heart; and boy of my dreams.